Cactus Mac   Bob

Bronco   Dona

Linda Craig

and the Secret

of Rancho del Sol

Linda Craig
and the
Secret of
Rancho del Sol

Ann Sheldon

DOUBLEDAY & COMPANY, INC.

GARDEN CITY, NEW YORK

1963

Contents

Linda Craig

and the Secret

of Rancho del Sol

I

Mystery Message

Linda ran into the ranch house living room waving a letter she had picked up from the mailbox.

"Bob," she said excitedly to her brother, who was reading, "this is addressed to you and me. It's from the Trail Blazers! Do you suppose it could be an invitation to join the club?"

"A good way to find out would be to open it," Bob replied, grinning. He was fair-haired and brown-eyed, favoring the Scottish strain of their father, while Linda had the brunette Spanish coloring of their mother.

Eagerly Linda slit open the envelope and pulled out a Trail Blazers Club 28 letterhead bordered with sketches of horses.

"This *is* an invitation to join!" exclaimed Linda joyfully. "That is, if we can qualify."

Bob beamed. "We'll work hard to. The committee doesn't take new members into the Trail Blazers every

9

day. They've evidently been watching our riding and noted our show awards—especially yours and Chica's."

Linda smiled at the thought of Chica d'Oro, her prized golden palomino filly, whom she had trained herself.

She read on: "'Meetings follow potluck suppers the second Thursday of each month.' What fun!"

"Thursday is day after tomorrow," said Bob. "Say, look at the large print at the bottom of the page: 'TRAIL RIDES. HORSE SHOWS. POSSE AIDES.'"

"Oh, isn't it marvelous!" Linda exclaimed. Then she frowned slightly. "Bob, do you suppose this Posse Aides category means that we'll be chasing *criminals?*"

"I doubt it. I think our part will be to track down clues to a culprit's identity, then let the sheriff do the capturing."

Sister and brother sat down to discuss the invitation in the comfortable, Spanish-style, beam-ceilinged room. It was in the Rancho del Sol, home of their grandparents, Tom and Rosalinda Mallory. Some months before, Linda and Bob Craig had lost both their father and mother in an accident in Hawaii where Major Craig had been stationed. Sixteen-year-old Linda and eighteen-year-old Bob had come to Rancho del Sol in the San Quinto Valley of southern California to live with the Mallorys. The young Craigs affectionately called them Bronco and Dona.

Having spent all their summers on the ranch, Linda and Bob felt at home here and loved their grandparents. To assuage their recent grief, the brother and sister had done a good deal of riding and had solved some local mysteries.

The ringing of the telephone interrupted their conversation. Linda answered.

"It's Kathy," she told Bob. Then she laughed happily. "Kathy received an invitation to join the Trail Blazers too!"

Kathy Hamilton was Linda's best friend, a gay honey-blonde of sixteen who had a pinto named Patches. Her parents owned the Highway House, a landmark on the desert highway. It combined snack bar, souvenir store, and lapidary shop. Here Mr. Hamilton cut, polished, and sold semiprecious stones. It was a mecca for local rock hounds.

Presently Linda hung up. "Kathy knows a lot about the Trail Blazers," she told Bob. "There are sixty clubs in the group. Number 28 has the reputation for being the most active and the most fun. Number 6, the Malibu coast group, is the wealthiest and ritziest. That is the one a girl named Shirley Blaine belongs to."

"And who is she?" Bob asked.

Linda shrugged. "Kathy said Shirley is the one I'll really have to watch out for in show contests. She's excellent, but hard to get along with. It seems that her one ambition in life is to qualify for the Olympic team and she lets everyone know this."

"Wow! That's some ambition," Bob remarked.

"And one that requires not only the tops in mounts and riding ability, but also the money to see it through," Linda reminded him. "I may never meet her, though. I'll have to qualify for the club before going against her in competition."

"Does that worry you?" Bob grinned.

"If she can beat me, it's fair enough," replied Linda with a tilt of her chin.

Again the telephone rang. Bob answered this time, saying, "Hi, Larry!" After a moment's conversation, he cried, "Great!" and nodded to Linda's question, "Trail Blazer invitation?"

Larry Spencer was Bob's chum, eighteen also, a tall, easygoing, brown-eyed youth whose father owned the leather goods and saddlery shop in the nearby town of Lockwood. Larry did not have a horse of his own, but rode one of the Rancho del Sol string.

On Thursday evening Linda and Bob drove to the Trail Blazers meeting and potluck supper in the Community Building at Tri-Canyon Junction. They carried a ham-and-lima bean casserole and a loaf of garlic sour dough bread.

Larry was waiting outside in his jeep. "Here's one of Mother's delicious devil's food cakes," he announced. Then Kathy drove in with a big bowl of salad.

The foursome was met by the president of the club, twenty-year-old Chuck Eller. He was a dark-haired, energetic athlete, whose commanding personality indicated the reason for the success of this particular club in the Trail Blazers.

"Hi, everybody!" he greeted them.

Sue Mason, his pretty, tawny-haired, hazel-eyed date, joined him, and took charge of the four proposed members to introduce them.

"You won't have any trouble passing the tests," she prophesied with a friendly chuckle, as she later left them.

It was a gala supper. Afterward, as soon as Chuck Eller had dispensed with routine business, he said, "Now we are ready to inform our four prospective members of their initiation. Our secretary will read the rules."

Sue Mason stood up with her book and began:

"'All new members are required to qualify by riding and blazing a new trail to some spot of exceptional or historical interest. They must bring back a report and snapshots of the place as well as of the new trail. When approved by the initiation committee, the new members will be privileged to join in all activities and missions of the club.'"

Linda, Bob, Kathy, and Larry glanced at one another with new excitement. The members grinned approvingly and clapped.

Chuck Eller arose and announced, "We have an important new mission to accomplish. Our members have been asked by the sheriff's office to act as an auxiliary posse and to help discover who or what, rustlers or wild animals, are causing the disappearance of cattle from small outlying ranches in this area. May I see hands of those who will be able to participate in this?"

Nearly every member raised his hand.

Chuck looked pleased. "Great! You'll all receive a bulletin on this as soon as we have worked out the details."

Linda whispered to her friends, "I'd like to participate. Do you suppose we can?"

They nodded eagerly and Bob asked Chuck, "May we receive copies?"

"Yes indeed."

As soon as the meeting was adjourned, Linda suggested to her group, "How about the four of us getting together at del Sol tomorrow to work out our initiation ride?"

The others agreed quickly and, the following afternoon, gathered on the secluded ranch patio, with its attractive redwood furniture and towering oak trees.

Rango, del Sol's yellowish-tan, coyote-shepherd dog, lay stretched out with one eye open, and

14

thumped his tail each time anyone spoke. He seemed aware that a riding trip was being planned, and aimed to do his best not to be left out of the fun.

Bob spread out maps of nearby sections.

"A lot of territory to choose from," Kathy remarked. "But where will we find an unblazed trail?"

"Here come two people who can help us," said Linda. "Dona and Bronco."

The fine-looking couple rode in on their horses and dismounted near the barn. Then they strode toward the patio. Both were tall and straight.

Dona Mallory, of Spanish origin, walked with a queenly gait. She was a beautiful, slender, olive-skinned woman, with dark graying hair worn in a chignon. Grandmother Mallory was always dignified and never deviated from her high ideals. Yet she joined easily in the fun and strange situations which arose at del Sol.

"I'm glad to see you," she said to Kathy and Larry. "We'll have tea and then suppose you tell me about your trip."

"We need advice," said Linda, as her grandmother went into the house to change from her riding clothes and ask the housekeeper to serve refreshments.

Bronco Mallory did not bother to change. He dropped his big frame into a lounge chair. "You folks got a world-shattering problem?" he teased.

When they told him, he scratched his iron-gray hair and twirled his big sombrero in mute answer to

15

the questions flung at him. He could think of no unbroken trail of historical interest. Dona Mallory returned, but she too could offer no solution.

At that moment Luisa Alvarez, Rancho del Sol's plump, genial Mexican housekeeper, brought out a tray of iced tea and gingerbread squares. When the nonplused group asked if she had any suggestions, the woman shook her head regretfully.

"Problems, always problems," she muttered, turning toward the kitchen.

Before entering it, Luisa looked toward a field where her two pet goats Geraldine and Genevieve were tethered. She called a cheery greeting to them in her native tongue, and waved her apron. Goat's milk was the only kind Luisa would use in her superb cookery.

"Here comes Cactus Mac," said Linda, seeing the lovable, bandy-legged ranch foreman. "Maybe he can suggest a place for us to go." She called out, "Paging Cactus Mac!"

The gray-haired man sauntered over, and with a broad smile asked drawlingly, "Who's in trouble now?"

"We all are," the young people answered.

Quickly Linda explained their problem and then said, "Mac, you know every inch of southern California, and about everything that has ever happened here. Where would you suggest that we ride?"

The foreman squinted his eyes in thought for a few

moments, then smiled cagily. "Wal, Crespi Cove should do it. Trailer your horses over to Scotty's Chuck Wagon Steak House on Valley Highway, and leave the outfits thar. Then break a trail over the hills to the Cove on the ocean. You'll find a historical marker right plumb on the sand."

"What is it?" asked Kathy excitedly.

"You'll learn when you get thar," Cactus replied and went on to the corral.

Linda laughed. "Well, I guess nothing will keep us from Crespi Cove to find out what's on that marker."

She and her friends made plans to leave early the following Monday.

"That's a long, hard ride. Take plenty of provisions," Bronco advised, and Dona added, "And blankets. It may be chilly at night."

The next morning Bronco left for a stock auction that would take him away from Rancho del Sol for an overnight stay. After Linda had said good-by to him, she went to feed Chica. How beautiful the golden palomino was, Linda thought. The two-year-old had a white mane and tail, four white stockings, and very intelligent brown eyes.

"I'll be back to give you a workout in a little while, baby," said Linda, and hurried off to make her bed and tidy her room.

When she returned to the barn, Linda found the filly standing with her head down in one corner of the stall.

17

"What's the matter, baby?" the girl asked with concern. "Why aren't you out in the sunshine?"

Chica lifted her head and whinnied a weak greeting. Presuming that she had just been taking a nap, Linda saddled the horse and took her out into the adjoining ring.

Almost immediately Linda became aware that Chica was limping badly with her hind legs. Her young rider dismounted hastily and examined each hind foot. Both were clean. But Chica seemed to be in considerable pain.

Terrified, Linda started to lead the palomino slowly back to her stall. Frantically she called, "Cactus Mac!"

He came running from the big barn, took one look at Chica, and barked, "Get the doc!"

Linda ran to the barn phone and called the veterinarian, Doctor Sawyer, in Lockwood. He reached the ranch within the hour. Linda stood by Chica petting and talking soothingly to her as he made an examination. Cactus Mac and Bob waited nearby for the diagnosis.

Doctor Sawyer examined Chica's feet and legs. Suddenly he exclaimed, "Wal, I'll be—this horse's legs have been threaded!"

"Wh-what do you mean?" gasped Linda.

"A thread has been pulled through her legs here above the hocks. It's affecting the nerves." Doctor Sawyer shook his head. "Haven't run onto this for years. It was an old-time race track trick to put a horse out of the running. This is a criminal offense."

He went to work pulling out the threads and treating the legs with a soothing medication.

"Will Chica be all right?" asked Linda fearfully.

"She will now," declared the veterinarian. "Just give her a few days rest. But if we hadn't found these threads now, your horse likely would have gone permanently lame."

"Who could have done this?" cried Linda angrily. "And why?"

She, Bob, and Cactus Mac searched for strange horse or tire tracks that might indicate someone had ridden into the ranch from the side or back. But they could find none.

"How did the person get here? On foot?" Linda asked, but no one could answer her.

Two deputies arrived from the sheriff's office where Doctor Sawyer had stopped to report the criminal incident. At the total lack of evidence or clues, one declared, "This must have been an inside job." He turned to Cactus Mac. "You'd better make a close check of your hands."

Cactus Mac bristled. "Ain't a one o' them what's that kind o' crackpot," he retorted.

With Chica now standing quietly, and needing a rest rather than a workout, Linda went into the house. It was a custom of hers to hesitate a moment in the hallway before the large oil portrait of her great-great-grandmother Rosalinda Perez who had come from Spain as a bride with her rich young grandee husband to Rancho del Sol, a grant to him from the Spanish king.

Linda strongly resembled her lovely ancestor, having the same fine features, glossy black hair, lustrous brown eyes, and creamy complexion.

"Oh, you are so exquisite in your Spanish wedding dress!" Linda said softly.

As she stood staring at the portrait, Bob came rushing into the hall. "Better go see what's bothering Chica now. She seems upset."

Linda lost no time. She ran all the way to the palomino's stall, followed by her brother. The filly was restive and nickering nervously. She settled down immediately, however, at sight of Linda.

"It's all right, sweetie," Linda crooned. "Nothing else is going to happen to you. I'll stay right here with you day and night."

"Suppose I take the night shift," Bob offered.

At that moment Linda's eye caught sight of something wedged between the feedbox and the stall side.

She snatched it out, examined the paper, then exclaimed, "What a strange message this is!"

II

Stranger on the Trail

"A strange message?" Bob repeated, reaching for the paper in his sister's hand.

"Better be careful," warned Linda. "This must be very old, it's so fragile—and the ink is faded. I think it's part of a letter. And look!" She held out the paper for Bob's inspection. "What odd spelling!"

The Craigs read the message together:

"*Famly chest holds secret. Dying wishe of the mistress is for faithful servants to share the tresur.*"

Bob glanced up at his sister, mystified. "Say!" he exclaimed. "This is a real poser."

"It sure is," agreed Linda. "I can't imagine who left the paper here, or why, or what it means."

Cactus Mac, passing by, noted the Craigs puzzling over the scrap of paper. "What have you young 'uns got thar?" he asked, entering.

Linda showed him the old stained scrap of paper with its mysterious message. Cactus Mac whistled.

21

Then he declared, "The varmint what threaded Chica must have left it here!"

Linda looked bewildered. "I don't see any connection."

"Me either," said Bob. "But there seems to be a lot happening around here that we don't understand!"

"We'd better be discovering fast what it's all about," said Linda determinedly.

"Check," Cactus Mac growled.

"Why do you suppose Rango didn't bark if a stranger came in?" Linda wondered. "By the way, where is he? Has something happened to *him?*"

"Not to that cheesehound," replied Cactus with a grin. "Rango's over t' the south acreage with Bud, who's clearin' out weeds and tryin' to persuade Vagabond to haul 'em off in a cart. You know how all-fired stubborn that donk is. Won't do a lick o' work 'cept for someone he likes."

Linda smiled, recalling how Chica d'Oro had found the hapless little donkey alone on the desert one night when she and some companions were on a cattle-trailing mission. The palomino and burro had become constant companions, with Rango running a close second in their affection.

Cactus Mac scowled. "But you can safely bet your last cent it was some crackpot stranger pussyfootin' around here. 'Tweren't none o' my crew."

"At any rate," Linda said, "I'd like to show this

note to Dona if one of you will stay with Chica."

"I aim to go further," said Cactus Mac. "I'll put her in a stall in the big barn. Me or one o' the men will keep an eye onto her so's you won't have to bother."

"All right," said Linda. "Thanks."

She took the note inside the ranch house. Dona perused it with deepening perplexity. "This message is strange indeed," she remarked.

Suddenly Linda burst out, "Do you suppose the family chest mentioned in this note refers to Rosalinda Perez's?"

She and Dona went into the hall and stood by the handsome carved black walnut chest standing beneath the oil portrait. Inside it were Rosalinda's wedding dress and accessories.

"If the note means this chest," suggested Linda excitedly, "then the secret mentioned might refer to the jewels!" She recalled again the story of the disappearance of Rosalinda Perez's fortune in jewels.

Dona Mallory shrugged. "As you know, they are not in the chest, dear. It has been thoroughly searched many times, and even tapped for a hidden compartment."

Linda looked up at her ancestor's portrait. "If you could only tell us what you did with them!" she murmured.

The jewels had apparently been hidden at the time when Captain Frémont, in 1846, had led a march on

California, which then belonged to Mexico, in an attempt to gain that territory for the United States. The Spanish ranchers, terrified by tales of the robbing and plundering by avaricious soldiers, had secreted their valuable possessions, particularly gems. Rosalinda Perez had done this also.

Soon after the war Señora Perez had lapsed into a serious illness, and had died without revealing the hiding place of the jewels. The house and gardens had been thoroughly searched by each succeeding generation occupying the ranch, but the gems had not been found.

It had long since been concluded by most of the family that the soldiers must have found the jewels and taken them. A few believed that perhaps Rosalinda had managed to send them back to her relatives in Spain.

"Do you suppose, Dona," Linda speculated, "that there actually could be a descendant of an old Perez servant who knows something about the treasure— and he's one of Bronco's new cowmen?"

"It seems improbable, after all these years," mused Dona. "But if so, he is doomed to disappointment believing the jewels are in this chest."

"Just the same," Linda said, "I think I'll go ask Cactus Mac about the new hands." She raced outside and spotted the foreman coming from the big barn.

In response to Linda's query, he said, "No, ma'am. There ain't one of my regular bunch, old or new, who considers himself a servant like that note says. Self-respectin' cowmen, that's what they are, and if those smart-aleck young lawmen come around here again badgerin' 'em with false accusations, they'll have me to reckon with."

Bob, who had begun to mend tack nearby, spoke up. "If there is such a 'faithful servant' character, why doesn't he show himself? And what has he got against Chica?"

"I just *can't* figure out the connection," Linda said, "although the message must have been left in Chica's stall this morning when her legs were threaded."

Bob shrugged in puzzlement. "All I know is, this mystery is making me hungry." He glanced at his watch and exclaimed, "No wonder! It's half an hour past lunch time!"

"Are you sure the outdoor bell didn't ring?" Linda asked him.

"Would I be here starving to death if it had?" Bob retorted with a chuckle.

"Not you," Linda admitted, laughing. "I'd better go see if Luisa needs any help."

Bob followed his sister into the kitchen. The room was filled with the strong odor of burned food.

"Goodness! What happened?" Linda asked the housekeeper.

"Oh, the lunch, it is all burned, all spoiled!" Luisa lamented. "My Genevieve, for some reason she go off yesterday and not come back last night. My Geraldine is so lonesome she won't eat or drink, and does not give much milk."

Luisa was distractedly walking around in a circle with the big baking dish of scorched food in her hands.

Linda took the dish from her and put it on the drainboard. "Don't you fret about lunch," she said kindly. "I'll fix something. You go out in the patio now and cool off."

Gently she propelled Luisa toward the door. "And don't worry any more about Genevieve. As soon as Bob and I have eaten we'll ride out and bring her back. She's probably not very far away."

Somewhat calmed down, Luisa complied.

Linda and Bob ate lunch quickly. Directly afterward they went out to get horses and go after the missing goat. Linda caught a cow pony named Brownie in the field and brought him into the barn to saddle.

While fastening the girth and shortening the stirrups, she talked to Chica d'Oro, now in the protective barn stall. Instead of appearing pleased, the palomino whinnied plaintively and pawed with a forefoot. Then she reached out with her nose and gave a quick hard push to Brownie's side, making him whirl.

Linda jumped out of the way. "What's the matter?" Then she laughed. "Why baby, you're jealous!"

She went to Chica and stroked the filly's neck to

calm her. "Brownie isn't replacing you, sweetie," Linda crooned softly. "He is only going to pinch-hit for you today on a short ride while your legs get well." The palomino seemed mollified and nuzzled the girl with her soft nose.

Old Bart, a del Sol hand of long standing, came out of the feed room with a molasses cake. "You go on, now," he said to Linda. "I'll take Chica's mind off bein' left behind by givin' her a little sweetenin'."

Linda flashed him a grateful smile and led Brownie outside, where Bob waited on his bay, Rocket. The Craigs picked up the missing goat's little tracks and followed them for some distance. They led up a draw, then disappeared.

"Oh, dear!" Linda sighed. "Where can Genevieve have gone?"

She and Bob leaned low from their horses, attempting to spot the tracks again. Suddenly a lone rider loomed up on the trail ahead of them.

In a low, concerned voice Linda said to Bob, "Where ever did he come from?" Bob shook his head, sitting straight and alert.

The rider, who was a medium-built man of about forty, approached the brother and sister.

"Howdy!" he greeted them. "I'm Rod Coleman. I've located on a ranch near here, and am just out for a little ride to get acquainted with the valley."

His friendly manner somewhat relieved Linda of any apprehension, and she replied pleasantly, "We're

Linda and Bob Craig from Rancho del Sol. We're looking for our housekeeper's goat. Have you seen a stray one?"

Coleman gave the girl a slow broad smile and replied, "As a matter of fact, I did notice one about a mile from here. If you like, I'll ride along with you and show you the spot. Glad to have company."

"Thank you very much," said Bob. "We'd appreciate that."

The trio turned up the draw. Linda and her brother kept listening for Genevieve's bell, but failed to hear it. Finally the riders came to a cabin. It was set close against the slope, which was thickly covered with ironwood trees and blooming wild buckwheat.

Linda and Bob looked questioningly at Rod Coleman. "Is this the place?" Linda asked.

Coleman appeared baffled at the absence of the goat and replied, "That's right. Say, you might knock at the door there, and inquire."

Linda and Bob exchanged cautious glances. Bob did not dismount and knock, but rode closer. "Hello, in there!" he called out.

The cabin door opened. Framed in the entrance was a tall, uncouth, cadaverous-looking man. He stared surlily at the Craigs.

"We're sorry to bother you," said Bob politely, "but we've lost a goat. We were told it was near here. Did you notice it?"

The man ran his tongue over his thin lips, and said, "Light, and come in."

"No, thank you," said Linda hastily. "We'd better keep searching for the goat."

Behind them Rod Coleman suddenly ordered, "Dismount and go in!"

The Craigs swung their horses to stare at him. Linda gasped. In Coleman's hand was a revolver, leveled on her and Bob! Every trace of geniality had left the man's face.

"Do as I say!" he ordered them. "Off your horses, and into the cabin!"

III

Ransacked Ranch House

Shocked and amazed, Linda and Bob sat tensely on their horses. As Linda looked down the barrel of the gun which Coleman held trained on them, she tried not to tremble.

"What is this all about?" Bob demanded. "We have nothing of value on us. You must have mistaken us for other people."

"No mistake," growled Coleman. "We're not going to hurt you. Just want to keep you here while we go to investigate something. But if you don't listen—"

"Ride out fast, Linda," said Bob quickly in a low voice, and clicked his heels to Rocket's flanks. But at that instant Rod Coleman, overhearing, fired into the air to show them he meant business.

Both Brownie and Rocket reared, then the panicked cow pony took off on a run down the draw. Linda started to pull him in, not wanting to leave Bob alone. But she heard him yell:

"Go on! Go on!"

The next moment she also heard pounding hoofs gaining on her, and Rod Coleman shouting, *"Stop!"*

When Linda did not rein in, there came a terrifying gun explosion, and the whiz of the bullet. Brownie screamed, and went down on his knees.

Linda sprang free. Almost immediately Brownie struggled to his feet, so she knew in relief that a bone had not been pierced by the bullet. She did see blood running from the cow pony's shoulder, and snatched out her handkerchief to press it against the wound.

"Easy, boy," Linda whispered. Her dark eyes flashed with outrage at Rod Coleman as he came alongside. "What kind of fiend are you to shoot a horse?" she cried.

"You do as I say, girlie, or you'll feel the next one!" he replied. "Get going back to the cabin and no more funny tricks."

With prickles running up and down her spine, and one hand clutching the end of Brownie's reins, Linda reluctantly obeyed. Bob was off Rocket and standing beside him. Linda, dismayed, immediately saw why he was there—the tall gaunt man in the cabin held a rifle!

Swiftly Rod Coleman dismounted. He left all the horses ground-hitched, then pushed Bob and Linda inside the building. Bob turned furiously and struck out at Coleman with knotted fists.

31

With an ugly leer the other man raised his rifle menacingly and snarled, "Back off!" Linda and Bob froze.

Coleman grabbed up a length of strong cotton rope that apparently had been used for a clothesline at some time. He cut lengths from this and bound the Craigs' wrists and ankles. Now he turned to a gun-rack on the wall. It had been constructed of old horseshoes, bolted sidewise to the wall, to hold guns or other heavy objects. Coleman tied ropes around Linda's and Bob's waists and fastened the line to the horseshoes, placing the prisoners in standing position a good six feet apart.

"So Bob and I can't help each other escape!" Linda thought grimly.

Rod Coleman stood before them arrogantly and said, "We'll turn you loose tomorrow. In the meantime my pal here and I are going to search the del Sol ranch house until we find those jewels your fancy Spanish lady ancestor hid."

Linda drew in her breath. "You won't find them. They're gone."

"That's what you think. But you're wrong."

The girl's eyes flashed as a thought came into her mind. "You're the one who left that piece of an old letter in my horse's stall!" she accused.

"Now you're getting smart." Coleman chortled by way of acknowledging this.

"But why," asked Linda, "if you intended to rob the ranch house, did you leave a clue like that?"

"Just an old trick to confuse the lawmen." Coleman grinned enigmatically. The gaunt man gave a harsh laugh. "It ought to work—or my name isn't Hank Trask—" He broke off suddenly as if he had not meant to identify himself.

"Where did you get that note about the jewels?" Bob prodded.

"Just you keep guessing on that one," Trask sneered.

Linda set her jaw. "You must be the same person who threaded my horse's legs," she accused Rod Coleman.

"One and the same," he admitted with a note of swagger in his tone as if proud of his achievement. "But next time—"

"Shut up!" barked Hank Trask.

Coleman gave his pal a displeased look, but closed his lips in a hard straight line.

"Why did you do such a heartless thing? Why?" Linda cried out. "And how did you get to the ranch?"

Coleman remained silent, except to say he had come on foot. He shoved a wooden chair in front of Linda, put a pan of water on it, and dumped out some crackers from a box. Then he pushed another chair before Bob and supplied it equally.

"Eat hearty!" Trask guffawed. The Craigs eyed him coldly and made no response.

The two men turned abruptly and went out, slamming the door hard after them. The strenuous jar, however, caused the door to rebound from the rusty old catch and stand open a couple of inches. It sagged badly onto the floor.

Through the crack Linda and Bob saw the men ride out, taking the Craigs' horses with them. They pulled the limping Brownie along mercilessly.

Anger flushed the faces of both brother and sister who strained desperately at their ropes. But the two soon realized with sinking hearts that they had been well secured.

Linda made a wry face at the crackers and water. "At least these men don't intend us to die of thirst or hunger. And probably they wouldn't have shot us. We should have fought harder to get away and made a dash for it on foot."

Bob shook his head. "They didn't intend to let us escape. If necessary they would have wounded us slightly to prevent it. What I'd like to know is how Rod Coleman and Trask found out about the Perez jewels."

As a sudden thought came to Linda, she shuddered. "Bob, those awful men are headed for del Sol. With Bronco still away, Dona and Luisa will be alone in the ranch house. They're in danger! And we can't do one thing to help them!"

The Craigs were sunk in gloom, fears for those at the ranch racing through their minds.

"If Rango has come back to the house, he'll go straight for those men," Bob conjectured hopefully.

"But they might shoot him!" Linda answered worriedly.

"I doubt it," said Bob, trying to reassure her. "The sound of a shot would bring in Cactus Mac or any of the men who might be nearby." To himself Bob added, "Those crooks might knock Rango out with a blow on the head, though."

"Oh dear," said Linda as a new worry assailed her. "If Cactus Mac should go into the house, what chance would he have against two guns?"

"Mac has dealt with rustlers and other outlaws," Bob reminded Linda. "He won't take any foolhardy chances—count on that!"

After a few minutes of silence, Linda said, "I just cannot figure out the other mystery—why Rod Coleman tried to put Chica d'Oro out of commission."

"Right now I can't figure that either," Bob admitted. "One thing's certain. He and his pal Hank Trask seem to be involved in more than one line of skulduggery."

The Craigs fell silent once more, their thoughts somber. As the hours passed, they caught themselves listening for sounds of the outlaws' return. No one arrived.

Darkness fell. With it came the usual night sounds

—the eerie call of the killdeer, the whoo of an owl, the scurrying of small animals, and the crack of twigs under the paws of larger creatures.

Linda had half-dozed. Suddenly she gave a start. "Bob, are you awake? Could that be a wildcat I hear out there?" she asked worriedly. "It may come in and attack us!"

"I'm plenty awake," replied Bob. "It may have been a wildcat, but lucky for us the door is hanging heavy on those hinges. I doubt if a cat would be cute enough to push it open."

The Craigs kept an uneasy vigil for the remainder of the night. With the first gray light of dawn Linda exclaimed, "Maybe Coleman and Trask don't intend to come back! I'm going to call for help. Someone might be out herding." She yelled several times, but there was no response.

"I'll give it a try," said Bob, and shouted lustily.

Suddenly Linda said, "Listen! I thought I heard a dog bark."

"I did too," said Bob. "Some kid with his dog may be out rounding up strays." He repeated the call for help.

The barking became louder and nearer. Linda called excitedly. As the dog barked again, she thought there was a joyous note to it.

"Why, that sounds like Rango!" she exclaimed, and cried out, "Here Rango! Here Rango!"

36

In a few moments the familiar big yellow head appeared at the crack of the door.

"Hi, boy!" Bob grinned in relief. "Come in and get us out of here."

Getting in was no problem for Rango! He shoved his big strong paw in the crack and pushed the door back. Then he bounded inside.

"Oh, Rango!" Linda laughed. "You great big wonderful beautiful darling! Here, chew this rope off." She thrust her bound wrists toward him.

Rango went to work quickly with his teeth. Chewing a binding rope from a person or an animal was one of the early training tricks Cactus Mac had taught Rango in order to make him a good working ranch dog.

"What do you suppose made Rango come looking for us?" Linda asked.

"My guess is that Cactus Mac sent him, as soon as he found we were missing," replied Bob.

When Linda's hands were free she untied her ankles, and with Rango's further help released the rope tied around her waist and fastened to the wall horseshoe behind her.

Then the girl and the dog together quickly freed Bob. He and Linda were both so cramped and sore that they could hardly move. But they massaged and flexed their arm and leg muscles until most of the stiffness was gone.

The Craigs hurriedly walked back to the ranch

house with Rango following. When it came into view they approached cautiously. Everything seemed ominously quiet.

"I hope nothing dreadful has happened," Linda said worriedly.

With anxious bravado she and her brother raced into the kitchen.

"Oh!" Linda stiffened and screamed.

Dona and Luisa sat tied to chairs with dishtowels, gagged. Their eyes were wells of terror. Linda and Bob hastily freed the women and asked who had bound them.

At first Luisa could only wring her hands and wail, "*O mio! O mio!*"

Dona took a deep breath and stood up, mustering her usual dignity and composure. "What a dreadful ordeal!" she murmured. Then, before telling her story, she looked anxiously at Linda and Bob. "I'm so thankful you are back! What happened? Where have you been?"

"Tied up in an old cabin by two men who wanted to keep us away from here," Bob informed his grandmother. "We were decoyed on the trail by one of them who posed as a new rancher neighbor."

"But Rango found us," Linda added.

Dona and Luisa were horrified over what had happened, and beamed at Rango as Linda patted the big dog. Rango curved his lips in a grin, and ran his tongue out in happy appreciation.

"We know the names of the two men who captured us," Linda declared.

"Three men came here," said Dona. "Three masked men."

"Three?" Bob repeated in surprise. "Was one tall, and another of medium height?"

"Yes," Mrs. Mallory replied. "And the third was medium height also, but a little huskier."

"Rod Coleman and Hank Trask picked up a confederate somewhere on the way to del Sol," Linda reasoned. "They must belong to a band of outlaws."

Bob added, "The two men we know as Coleman and Trask said they were coming here to search for Rosalinda Perez's jewels. Did they?"

"Yes," Dona replied, pained by the recollection. "Those—thieves announced they had come for the Perez treasure, and ransacked the entire house. We heard them going from room to room. I don't know what they may have taken."

Linda and Bob ran into the hall and stared in dismay at the open carved chest. The beautiful white satin brocade wedding dress and all the accessories were strewn about the floor. Linda's eyes filled with tears.

Then she and her brother gasped as they peered into the chest. "There *is* a false bottom!" Bob exclaimed. "And it has been forced open!"

"The jewels!" Linda cried out. "Rod Coleman found the jewels!"

IV

The Captured Foreman

Dona, who had hurriedly joined Bob and Linda in the hallway, looked astounded.

"I never heard that there was a false bottom in the Perez chest," she declared, "or that the jewels were there. It has been thoroughly examined in the past for hidden compartments, so I am sure the gems would have been found."

Linda was not convinced that the three masked men had not succeeded in finding the jewels. "Since they had the old letter, they might have obtained further information from some source."

"That is possible," her grandmother conceded. "But I shall keep hoping the thieves went away empty-handed."

"We'll do our best to find out," Bob said grimly.

"And now"—Mrs. Mallory moved along the hallway with quiet dignity—"I wish to make certain the vandals have not damaged our home any further."

Linda quickly put a hand on her grandmother's arm. "Oh, please, Dona, not now. You're very brave, but I know you and Luisa are exhausted from your dreadful experience. I'll make us all some hot bouillon, then won't you two go to bed and rest?"

Mrs. Mallory was finally persuaded, and Linda had the hot drink ready in a few minutes. After they had finished it, the women went upstairs.

"I'm going on a tour of inspection," Bob told his sister, "and see if anything else is missing, and if those crooks left any clues to establish their guilt."

"Good," said Linda. "Meanwhile, I'll begin downstairs and straighten up some of the jumble they made tearing this place apart."

When Bob had completed his check, he reported to Linda, "Those men sure turned things upside down and inside out. But nothing seems to have been taken except money from purses, and my collection of old coins is gone."

"What a shame!" said Linda sympathetically. "Did you find any evidence that could be used against them?"

"No. I'm going outside now and look around. And I'd like to talk to some of the ranch hands."

"I'll keep on with my job here," said Linda.

Bob went to the bunkhouse and stood inside the door astounded. No one was there, and not a bed had been slept in, including that of Moe, the cook.

"Very peculiar," Bob told himself with a frown. He

wondered what had come up to keep the men and the chuck wagon out on the range overnight. They usually came in every evening.

He hastened around to Cactus Mac's private quarters and discovered that the foreman's room too had not been occupied that night. Fearful for Chica d'Oro and the other horses, Bob ran to the barn. He stopped dead in the entrance, aghast.

Slumped against a bale of hay was Cactus Mac, trussed up and gagged with a piece of feed sack. Fearing that the foreman had been badly injured, Bob hurried to his side. Cactus seemed to be merely dozing, and when Bob touched his shoulder he snapped awake.

The wiry man struggled against his bonds and made muffled sounds of anger. Bob quickly took off the gag and untied the ropes.

The foreman got up and stamped about for a few moments, berating his attackers. Then he stopped suddenly. "Say! What in tarnation happened to you and Linda?" he demanded. "Where've *you* been?"

"Trussed up like you—in an old cabin up a draw," replied Bob. "Rango tracked us down and freed us. Did you send him?"

"Nope. Never had a chance," Mac muttered. "Guess he figured somethin' queer was goin' on here and went after you."

Bob fully relayed Dona's story. "Linda and I know

42

the names of two of the men—the ones who tied us up. But we don't know who the third might be."

"Didn't hear any names mentioned," said Cactus. "But I saw that two were medium height, and one was tall."

Bob then asked, "Where are all the hands? None of them came back to the bunkhouse last night."

Cactus Mac frowned. "No reason for 'em to stay on the range now. I'll go check the bunkhouse."

"And I'll call the sheriff pronto," Bob said.

He started back to the house as the foreman strode away angry-faced. Bob gave Deputy Sheriff Randall complete details of everything that had happened to all of them, and the reason for the ranch house ransack. He described Rod Coleman and Hank Trask, giving their names, then told of the third man.

The officer speculated, "That third man was undoubtedly Rod's brother, Ben. They look alike, except that Ben's huskier. The Colemans and Trask are fast-buck operators who are wanted by the authorities."

"They can't be very far away yet," Bob guessed. "The men might have headed back to the cabin up the draw since they didn't know Linda and I escaped." He described the location of the cabin for Randall.

"Deputies will be sent there at once," the officer said grimly.

As Bob hung up, Linda walked in. She was as-

43

tounded to hear about the empty bunkhouse and the attack on Cactus Mac. A quick look of anxiety came over her face.

"Chica!" she cried. "With all the men gone, and Cactus tied up, who knows what else Rod Coleman might have done to my palomino?"

The Craigs raced out to the barn. "Chica!" called Linda, hastening straight to the inside stall at the rear of the building.

The horse was not visible. A lump rose in Linda's throat. Then she saw the golden filly in a shadowy corner with her head dropped. She was sleeping.

"Chica, baby, are you all right?" her young owner asked as she opened the door and went inside.

The filly tossed up her head with a glad nicker of welcome and stepped sprightly over to Linda.

"Oh, Chica, there's nothing wrong with you!" crooned Linda joyously, hugging her around the neck. Then she turned the palomino about, looking her over carefully. "Why, you're in good shape! Even your poor threaded legs seem well."

Bob, coming over to Chica's stall, said, "Colonel's all right. I just made a check." Colonel was Bronco's chestnut Morgan. "And what do you think? Brownie and Rocket are back!"

"Coleman and Trask left them here?" Linda exclaimed unbelievingly.

"They must have."

"And they're unharmed?"

44

"Apparently."

"Bob, I can't understand it," said Linda. "Why do those men have a grudge against Chica d'Oro?"

"Deputy Sheriff Randall said those three men are fast-buck artists. Does that mean anything to you?" Bob asked.

"You mean someone paid Coleman to harm Chica?" Linda surmised. "But *who?*" she asked.

"I can't even make a guess," her brother answered. "But the sheriff's men are moving in on that trio of crooks. If they catch up with them and are able to make them talk, then we'll know the reason and who's causing all the trouble."

"I hope it won't be long." Linda's eyes flashed.

A moment later Cactus Mac came back into the barn. "Can't figure out what's kept my hands away," he said. "Don't believe they were run off. The lot of 'em would be a match for those three masked coyotes."

Just then he and the Craigs noticed dust whirling high on the lane leading out to the range. A rider was coming in fast.

Cactus Mac squinted into the sunlight. "That's Lanky Thompson, one o' my men!"

In a few moments Lanky slid his horse to a stop on its heels in front of the group and jumped off. "Is everything all right here?" he asked in concern.

"Ain't nothin' all right here," growled Cactus Mac. "Why you askin'? Where've you all been?"

Lanky removed his hat and took a soiled note from the crown. He explained, "A stranger rode out on the range late yesterday and gave Pinky this note signed by you, Cactus. Pinky figured the man was a new rider you'd put on."

"What's it say?" barked Cactus.

Lanky read: "'Stay where you are until I join you. Cactus.'" He passed the paper over to the foreman.

"I never sent this note," muttered Cactus angrily. "This ain't my writin'."

"I guessed it wasn't the minute I saw the note," Lanky told him. "That's the reason I rode right in to see what was happening back here. I figured there was trouble."

"You figured right," said Bob.

"Do you know what that note-passin' joker looks like?" Cactus demanded.

"Pinky said he was medium-height and stocky, with brownish hair," replied Lanky.

"Sounds like Ben Coleman, Rod's brother," Linda guessed.

"Get a fresh horse," said Cactus to Lanky, "and go tell the men to bring the cattle close by and report in. And tell 'em any orders I give I'm a-sayin' 'em, not writin' 'em."

As Lanky went off, the foreman glanced at Linda, who was leaning wearily against the barn doorjamb. "You two better get some shut-eye," he advised.

46

"That's for me." Bob grinned. "I'm just about asleep on my feet."

"I *am* asleep," Linda admitted wryly.

The Craigs went quietly into the house and directly to bed. Some time later Linda was awakened by strong sunlight and a delicious aroma. She glanced at the clock. Quarter to twelve.

"Mm-m!" Linda sniffed slowly. "I wonder what unusual dish Luisa's concocting for lunch!"

After a brisk shower and a change of clothes, Linda felt refreshed and hurried from her room. She met Bob at the top of the stairway and said teasingly, "I'll bet you're heading for the kitchen, too!" She laughed. "Only food would bring you out of bed!"

"Right!" Bob admitted, chuckling. "Come on, let's investigate."

They raced into the kitchen. Luisa, looking like her cheerful self, was at the stove stirring the contents of a huge iron kettle. From it came a tantalizing odor.

"Luisa, whatever are you making that smells so divine!" Linda exclaimed. "Is it a new recipe?"

With a mysterious smile the housekeeper gestured toward the center worktable. On it was a big basket containing a variety of vegetables yet to be peeled —tomatoes, cucumbers, cabbages, celery, and red and green peppers. Alongside was a freshly pulled pile of herbs from Luisa's garden, and boxes of spices.

"Don't tell me that's our lunch!" Linda said, astounded at the size of the kettle.

The housekeeper laughed heartily. "Not lunch."

"It smells terrific," said Bob. "How about a sample?"

Luisa laughed again and gave him a sample. "It will taste better in about four weeks," she said.

"My goodness, what *is* this recipe?" Linda puzzled, as Bob made a face and said, "It bites!"

"You ask your grandmother," the Mexican woman replied, her eyes twinkling.

Mrs. Mallory was just coming into the kitchen. She appeared rested and, to the Craigs' relief, showed no ill effects from her harrowing experience.

"Ask me what?" Dona said, smiling at them all.

"The name of the special food that's cooking in the kettle," said Bob.

"This is Luisa's famous chili vinegar," Dona informed them. "She alone knows the recipe. It has been handed down in the Alvarez family from one generation to the next. And it will be Luisa's and my contribution to the Ladies' Guild's Benefit Fiesta Fair. The proceeds go to our community Children's Hospital."

"What a wonderful idea!" exclaimed Linda.

Luisa sighed. "Every year I fill more bottles, and there is never enough."

"I should think not," said Linda, "if it tastes as good as it smells."

"Do you have to cook and stir it day and night?" Bob teased.

"*O mio!* Men!" exclaimed Luisa, throwing up her hands. "It is cooled, and strained through cheese-cloth many times—that takes very long. Then it must stand in the bottles more time before using."

"I'll personally see that you and your bottles of chili vinegar arrive safely at your booth in the Fiesta," said Bob.

"*Gracias.*" Luisa beamed.

"Mind if I rustle up a piece of bread now for lunch?" he asked. "I have a powerful gnawing in my middle."

"For lunch you eat what I make for you," Luisa scolded. She opened the oven door, disclosing a baking dish of enchiladas in bubbling cheese sauce.

Dona, Linda, and Bob were soon seated in the dining room and enjoying the enchiladas and a mixed green salad. Dessert was chilled pineapple pudding.

When they had finished, Linda said, "Bob, I think we ought to start out again to look for Genevieve—although Luisa doesn't seem so upset about her today."

"She still misses the goat," said Dona. "But I called the Foster ranch, which keeps goats, to deliver a daily supply of milk here until Genevieve's return."

Mrs. Mallory's face clouded with worry. "Do you think it is safe for you two to go out again on the horses?"

"We'll be on our guard this time, Dona," Bob assured her. "And from what Randall told me, this valley will be swarming with deputies."

"I'll slip my police whistle into my pocket," said Linda. "And if I see anyone who even slightly looks like the Colemans or Trask, I'll start blowing it. That'll bring the officers fast!"

When Bob was again mounted on Rocket, and Linda on another cow pony from the work string, a chestnut named Jubilee, she asked, "Where to this time, brother?"

"I suggest we search around all the watering spots we know," replied Bob. "It's my guess we'll find Genevieve at one of them."

"Lead off," said Linda.

They looked without luck at a couple of water holes and a big concrete trough. Then the Craigs followed a cow path to an upper range. It was impossible, however, to pick up any small goat tracks in the maze of cows' hoofprints.

Linda and Bob stopped on a bench to rest their horses. They looked admiringly down on a pretty cove, well shaded with cottonwoods and scrub oaks, and with a small stream of water trickling from the rocks on the side hill. In a few moments they became aware that the cove was occupied. Linda pointed out a man, a woman, several children, a burro, and a tarp stretched for cover.

"Gypsies!" exclaimed Bob.

"I think they're Mexicans," said Linda. "That's a Mexican blouse the woman has on." Then she added excitedly, "And look under the canvas covering—isn't that a goat?"

"It sure is," replied Bob. "Well, what are we waiting for? Let's ride down and see if the nanny answers to the name of Genevieve!"

V

Mama Diaz's Warning

As the Craigs' horses slid down the hillside, the Mexican children scampered in all directions, disappearing behind brush and boulders. The woman shielded the goat with her ample frame as she untied its frayed tether rope and pushed the animal into the dense protection of a scrub oak.

The man, hardy-looking and muscular, stood impassive, his dark eyes dull.

"Hello," Bob said. "We're from a nearby ranch, and are out hunting a lost goat. We saw the one you have here and wondered if it is yours, or if it strayed into your camp."

Linda meanwhile was gazing about, amazed at how swiftly the rest of the family had vanished. She turned to the Mexican. "Everyone is gone," she said. "What's the matter?"

A flicker of fear gleamed in the man's eyes. He

shrugged, spreading his hands before him in a hapless gesture, and muttered, "No speeka English."

Linda and Bob exchanged understanding glances, and Bob repeated his questions about the goat in Spanish. He and his sister spoke the language fluently, as did each generation of del Sol occupants.

The Mexican was staring at the Craigs, baffled, his face saddening and shoulders drooping. Speaking in his native tongue, he said, "I cannot find work. Cannot pay rent. We had to leave our little house. We have only one sack of beans and some corn meal."

Linda and Bob dismounted, their faces filled with compassion.

"What is your name?" Linda asked.

"I am Pico Diaz, and this is my family," he said, waving a circling arm. Little brown, round-eyed faces began to peek out from the brush. "If the goat is yours—we did not know. We did not steal it."

"Did you find the goat?" asked Linda gently.

"Not find it either," replied Diaz. "Two men who look much alike—must be brothers—came to our camp with it. They asked for a meal. The wife made beans and corncakes for them. Then they left goat."

He clasped his hands as a momentary shine came into his eyes. "The nanny gives good milk for my little *niños*." He looked at the Craigs sadly again. "Is she yours?"

"We don't know for sure until we see her," said Linda. She called softly, "Genevieve. Genevieve."

53

There was an instant responsive bleating from behind the scrub oak, and Genevieve, pulling loose from the hold of Mama Diaz, came running out to Linda and Bob.

They petted her with welcoming happiness, and Linda exclaimed, "Oh Genevieve, are we glad to find you!"

Mama Diaz came forward and stood with one hand on the goat. "You take the nanny away?" she asked despondently in Spanish. "You take milk from my little ones?"

The children gathered around the goat and fondled Genevieve. Tears moistened the eyes of several of the youngsters, who spoke up almost in chorus:

"Nanny is ours."

"We like Nanny."

"We like Nanny's milk."

While Genevieve appeared pleased to see Linda and Bob, she seemed content in her new adoring circle. Linda looked helplessly at her brother.

Bob gave his head a slight perplexed shake, and changed the subject by asking the Mexicans, "The men who brought the goat here looked alike, you say?"

"Si," replied Pico Diaz.

"But one was bigger," offered Mama Diaz. "They rode such nice horses, a black one and a brown one."

"The Coleman brothers, all right!" Linda exclaimed.

"You know those men?" asked Mama Diaz in surprise.

"We are pretty certain we do," Linda replied. "They're bad men." She said to Bob in English, "Now I get the picture. The Colemans took Genevieve from the ranch that night to lure you and me away. They figured on handling Dona and Luisa easily. They knew we'd go riding off looking for the goat. That's why Rod Coleman was waiting for us on the trail."

Bob's forehead puckered. "What are we going to do about the goat? We can't give her away. And if we go back and ask Luisa, these people may disappear with Genevieve while we're gone."

"I don't think so," Linda said. "I believe the Diazes are thoroughly honest. Just down, way down on their luck." She suddenly brightened. "Perhaps we could find a job for Papa Diaz!"

"That's a good idea," said Bob.

"If we tell the family that, and leave Genevieve here, they would be sure to wait for us to come back with the good news," Linda went on.

"Terrific brainstorm, sis! We'll do just that!" Bob exclaimed.

When the Craigs imparted this decision to the Diazes, the Mexicans' sad and tearful faces were immediately wreathed in smiles.

"We will be very good to the nanny," said Mama Diaz.

"We like Nanny!" cried the children again, hopping merrily about Genevieve.

Bob took all the money he had from his pocket and handed it to Pico Diaz. "Ride out to the store on your burro and bring back food for your family," he suggested.

With a broad smile Pico Diaz vigorously nodded his head in gratitude, and Mama Diaz reiterated, *"Gracias! Gracias!"* and kissed first Linda, then Bob, who blushed a bright red.

The Craigs waved and set off at top speed for the ranch. As soon as they had arrived, unsaddled, and cared for their horses, Linda checked on Chica d'Oro. The palomino was still all right, but pacing restlessly against her confinement.

"Tomorrow you get out, my rambunctious beauty," Linda promised, stroking the filly fondly.

The two young people hastened toward the house. They had just reached the door when a familiar deep voice hailed them.

"Bronco!" Linda cried as her grandfather strode up to them, saying he has just returned.

After an affectionate exchange of greetings Bob asked, "How did the stock-buying trip go?"

"Fine. Real fine," Mr. Mallory replied.

In a few minutes the entire family were convened

in the living room. Luisa served mugs of cinnamon-spiced Mexican hot chocolate.

"Any news here?" Bronco asked, relaxing in his big leather chair.

Receiving no answer to his question, the rancher sat forward and looked from face to face in concern. "What's wrong? Something has happened. I can sense it."

Dona spoke up. "Linda, suppose you tell your grandfather what has taken place here, since it all started with Chica d'Oro."

"All right," said Linda, drawing a long breath. "But the rest of you please help me."

When she finished her harrowing story, Bronco's face became grim. He vehemently slapped both chair arms with his broad hard palms, and got to his feet.

"This has gone too far! I think I'll offer my services as a deputy and hunt for those men myself!"

Dona looked at her husband admiringly but said, "Perhaps the sheriff's men have caught them already."

"May I put in the call?" Bob asked. "I want to report the Diaz story of the two men they saw."

"Go ahead."

When Bob returned, he said, "The sheriff's men haven't located the Colemans and Trask."

In the meantime Linda had told the others about the plight of the Diaz family. Now Bronco said, rubbing his hand over his thick, iron-gray hair, "I'll phone around right now—maybe I can get the man a picking job at one of the fruit ranches."

"Wonderful!" said Linda. "It would mean so much to them!"

In a short time Bronco announced that a pear orchard owner, Ed Runcie, could use some additional pickers, and would employ the Diazes if they would be steady workers.

"I'm sure they will be," said Linda. "And the older children can help pick."

Bob got up and excused himself. "I'd better start feeding the horses."

After he had gone, Bronco turned to Linda. "Runcie is coming right over," he said. "Perhaps you and I could take him out to the Diaz camp and bring the family back to a cabin on his ranch before dark."

"Oh yes," said Linda enthusiastically. "I'll show you the way."

When Mr. Runcie rode in, Linda and Bronco were waiting, their horses saddled. They led a bareback horse on which three of the Mexican children could sit.

When they arrived at the Diaz camp, Linda was struck by how different the scene was from the one earlier in the day. The children were skipping about in happy noisy games. Mama Diaz was singing a cheerful Mexican tune. On two planks laid across boxes was a kettle that had contained meat stew, and the remaining crumbs from a loaf of bread. Papa

Diaz had apparently lost no time in bringing back food for his hungry family.

"He seems dependable," Mr. Runcie commented in a low voice. Linda had informed him, on the way, of all the details she knew concerning the Diaz family.

The three dismounted, and Linda introduced Mr. Runcie and her grandfather to the Mexicans.

"I can use pear pickers on my ranch now," Mr. Runcie told them. "Would you like a job with me?" Linda translated the message.

Pico Diaz was shocked speechless with delight for a moment, but his face mirrored his gratitude. Finally, in a voice husky with emotion, he said in broken English, "I work good."

"Fine," said Mr. Runcie. "If so, you will be kept on after the pear crop is picked. There are always other jobs around my ranch for a hard worker."

Mama Diaz clasped her hands and went into a series of joyous exclamations in her native tongue.

One of the older girls asked, "Will we live in a house again?"

"Yes," Mr. Runcie smiled. "I provide good quarters for all my workers, including clean cots for everyone."

Mama Diaz's face suddenly grew somber. She beckoned Linda aside, and said in a low tone, "I must say something to you."

Concerned by her seriousness, Linda suggested quickly, "You will ride behind me then."

The Mexicans gathered together their few possessions. Mama Diaz, holding her family's extra clothes in a bundle, mounted the plank table and managed to clamber up behind Linda on Jubilee's rump.

Three little girls were lifted by Papa Diaz onto the unsaddled horse. Bronco and Ed Runcie each took two children on their saddles.

Pico Diaz had packed their table implements inside the cooking kettle, which he held in one hand. He stepped astride the burro, then loosened Genevieve's tether rope.

"All set? Let's go!" Mr. Runcie called out, and the strange-looking caravan started off.

Immediately Mama Diaz whispered in Linda's ear, "Those two men who gave us Nanny came back. They saw the food I was cooking and asked if someone had been to see us. I told them *si*, and explained what you look like."

The woman gave a worried sigh. "At first the men acted nice. But after I told them about you and your brother, they looked mad and talked loud. They rode off fast."

Linda shuddered. The Colemans and Trask apparently had not returned to the cabin up the draw, and thus had not known that she and Bob had escaped. "*Now* they've found out," she thought apprehensively.

Mama Diaz had been holding onto Linda for support. In agitation, the woman waved one hand, saying, "I am frightened they will try to do much harm to you and your nice brother."

Suddenly she started to slip sideways, and grabbed Linda tight around the waist again.

Linda said over her shoulder, "Don't worry. We will watch out for them."

At the Runcie ranch Linda took over Genevieve's lead rope, and Bronco that of the extra horse. There were no tears now from the Diazes at the prospects of losing Genevieve. The children kissed the goat good-by, and said, "Thank you for your nice milk."

The visitors from Rancho del Sol rode off. The instant Linda and Bronco arrived home, Luisa flew outside and gathered Genevieve in her arms.

Geraldine came bounding up and bleated her welcome. The two goats butted their heads together in happy reunion.

At that moment Bob came in from the back field and said, "I think we'd better lock everything up tight around here until those crooks are caught."

"No need," said Bronco. "I'm hiring armed guards to remain on this place. A couple are going on duty tonight." He hurried into the house, phoned the deputy sheriff's office, and confirmed his arrangements for the guards.

When the family were all together again in the living room, Linda reminded Bob, "We're supposed to get started on our Crespi Cove trip tomorrow morning."

"Do go," Dona put in. "It will get you away from this upsetting situation here."

Linda was immediately aglow with enthusiasm and suggested to Bob, "How about my calling Kathy and Larry to stay here tonight so we can get an early start? I'll help Luisa pack food."

Both friends eagerly accepted. After dinner Linda brought four saddlebags into the kitchen from the barn. With Luisa's efficiency, the bags were filled with canned and dry foods and bacon. Last of all, the Trail Blazers attest papers were carefully tucked in.

Later the Craigs laid out the sleeping bags and horse equipment which would be taken in the cars as far as Scotty's Steak House. Horse feed was loaded into the trailer saddle compartments. Next one trailer was hitched to the station wagon which Bob would drive.

When Larry arrived in his car, he greeted Linda and her brother with a grin. "Looks like a real safari!"

"Packed full of adventure!" Linda retorted.

The other horse trailer was hitched to his car. A few moments afterward Kathy rode in on Patches.

"Looking for work?" Bob asked her teasingly.

"No, sir," she flashed back. "I was raised a pet!"

He helped her put Patches away for the night in

the barn. By five next morning t
up and gathered for Luisa's
sausage and waffles.

Within half an hour the group
Rocket and Chica d'Oro were in
tached to Bob's station wagon.
with him. Patches and Jubilee follo\
trailer, to be drawn by Larry's car, v   ̣ated
beside him.

Bronco and Dona stood waving good-by. Between
them sat Rango, thumping his tail as if aggrieved at
being left behind.

As the four new Club 28 candidates drove along in
the bright crisp morning air, Linda sang snatches of
popular tunes, and Larry hummed along with a half-
smile on his lips. Suddenly, on the Durango Canyon
Road, which dropped steeply on both sides, the couple gave horrified gasps and Larry braked to as quick
a stop as he dared without throwing the horses.

The trailer ahead had lost a wheel and bumped
down on one side. It was rocking and weaving peril-
ously toward the steep embankment!

VI

Unfriendly Bear

Linda and Larry sat paralyzed as they saw the trailer ahead veer crazily toward the sheer drop. The wheel had already gone over the embankment.

"Bob—Kathy—Chica—they'll be—" Linda shut her eyes as if to close out the hideous thought.

At that moment she heard Larry exclaim "Whew! Thank heaven!"

Fearfully Linda opened her eyes. A feeling of relief swept over her. The car and horse trailer ahead had come to a slow bumping stop at the very edge of the cliff. Chica's stall was listing badly.

"Oh, I hope no one is hurt," Linda gasped.

She and Larry jumped out and ran to the disabled trailer. Bob and Kathy, white-faced, met them. "Are you two all right?" Linda asked them anxiously.

"Sure, sis. Just a little shaken up!" Bob assured her.

"Same for me," Kathy spoke up gamely.

The boys let down the tail gate and led the horses out, turning them in a circle.

"They seem to be all right," Bob observed.

"Except they're nicked some," said Kathy.

Linda carefully scrutinized the reddening spots on Chica d'Oro and Rocket. "Not bad," she diagnosed. "I'll get out some healing powder and put it on those spots before we load up again."

Chica, apparently considerably alarmed by the shake-up, was dancing and whinnying nervously.

Linda took the filly's tie rope from Larry. "I'll walk her up and down a bit to calm her."

Bob handed Rocket's rope to Kathy. Then he and Larry went off to slide down the embankment and retrieve the wheel. When they had hauled it back up to the trailer, Bob exclaimed, "The cotter pin and nut are gone!"

Larry made a grimace and frowned. "To the best of my knowledge, a cotter pin doesn't just come out of its own accord."

The girls had returned in time to pick up the gist of the conversation. "You mean you think somebody deliberately took it off?" Linda asked.

"Yes." Bob's face flushed with anger.

"Whoever would pull a horrible prank like that?" asked Kathy incredulously.

"I'd say that this wheel business is more than a prank," stated Bob flatly. "It could have been done by the same sneak who hired Coleman to harm Chica before. He would know this is her trailer because her name is on the side door."

"And it was probably done at the same time as the attack on Chica," Linda concluded. "The person wanted to be doubly sure she was harmed."

Larry was attempting to place the wheel back onto the axle. "If we can find the nut, it will probably hold the wheel on until we get to a garage."

Bob procured the repair kit and the girls searched the ground for the nut.

Kathy spoke up suddenly, "Here it is."

"Good!" said Bob and soon he and Larry had the wheel fairly secured in place. The boys borrowed a bobby pin from Kathy to replace the lost cotter pin.

Meanwhile Linda had dusted the horses' skinned spots with the healing powder. She loaded Rocket easily. But when she started to lead Chica inside, the palomino pulled back on the rope in stubborn refusal.

"Come on, baby," the girl coaxed. "We've lost too much time now." She tugged a little more forcibly on the rope, but Chica braced her legs on the pavement.

"Well!" Linda exclaimed. "Chica's never done this before." She took the filly a couple of paces, whirled her, and then ran toward the trailer. At the edge of the ramp Chica stopped suddenly and could not be budged. Larry picked up one of her forefeet and placed it on the boards. As soon as he set the palomino's other foot onto the plank, however, she backed off quickly.

"I'll try a blindfold," said Bob.

This ruse did not work either. Chica only jumped around from side to side, becoming more unmanageable.

Linda sighed. "I guess I'll just have to ride back home. The rest of you go on."

"Nothing doing!" Bob declared. "We stay together or we *all* return to the ranch until another time."

Suddenly Linda exclaimed, "I have it! You saw how Chica was thrown half down by the slant of the trailer floorboards when the wheel came off. She *might* be afraid that is how she'll have to stand in there now."

"You could be right," said Kathy slowly. "But how are we going to persuade her otherwise?"

"I know," said Linda quickly. "By putting Rocket in Chica's stall, and her into his."

They transferred Rocket. Then, with bated breath, Linda started to lead Chica into Rocket's place. The palomino walked right inside without hesitation.

"Pretty neat," said Larry. "Folks, meet the world-famous horsewoman!"

Bob grinned. "Jest bring yore hoss problems to trouble-shootin' Lindy Craig!" Sobering he asked, "Shall we go?"

When the four arrived at Scotty's Steak House, they were relieved to see a gas station a short distance further along with a small service garage. The mechanic there assured them he would fix the trailer wheel that very day.

The Craigs and their friends arranged to leave the outfits at the garage, and started to saddle up. They attached the bags of supplies, tied the bedrolls across the horses' flanks, and after filling the canteens at the station, tied them on with the front saddle strings. Sacks containing pellet horse feed were swung over each horn along with collapsible canvas water buckets.

"Okay, let's hit the trail!" Bob urged.

The club members mounted and rode into Cabrillo Canyon beyond whose hills lay the Pacific Ocean and Crespi Cove. The riders knew they must hit a direct but unbroken route to the cove. The road they were on ended at a poultry ranch. At this point they stopped and each took a compass from his pocket.

"Cactus Mac said we were to go due west from here," Bob advised. "Everybody get your direction, and when I say point, indicate the line we should follow up the slope." He waited a couple of moments, then said, "Point!" doing the same himself.

Each initiate's finger marked exactly the same direction up the sycamore- and laurel-covered slope.

"What you might call unanimous!" remarked Linda gaily.

Laughing, the four friends started upward, but Bob halted them again at the first big sycamore. He took a roll of wide adhesive tape from his pocket, tore off a small strip, and firmly attached it to the trunk. On the tape he wrote with a black grease pencil the large, heavy letters C-H-S.

"That's for Craig-Hamilton-Spencer," he announced. "Can't do any carving. It's against the forestry regulation—might kill the trees."

Larry brought out his camera. "I'd like to snap a picture here at the beginning of our trail," he said. "Look natural!"

"We'll try!" Kathy assured him. "Everybody say cheese."

As the riders proceeded, they found the going fairly easy. They all reached out and broke back the brush to establish the trail permanently. Bob left the initialed tape patches at intervals. Linda and Kathy, who both had small cameras slung around their necks, took an occasional snapshot.

In another hour they rode into pine country, and the ground became rough with occasional mounds of huge boulders. The underbrush lessened, but there was a thick carpet of dry pine needles on which the horses' feet slipped.

"We've really hit back country," Bob said.

"Smells good," Linda commented, breathing deep of the aromatic scented air.

The denseness of the forest obscured the sunlight, so Larry, who carried a supply of flashbulbs, took the pictures. The riders now had to consult their compasses frequently to keep on the right track.

Suddenly Chica stopped with her ears pricked forward. "What is it, baby?" asked Linda softly.

Signs of nervousness in the other horses caused their riders to pull them up short. Patches whirled, apparently intending to bolt back the way she had come, but Kathy held her in firmly.

Larry said in an undertone, "Look over there to the right!"

Following his pointing finger, the others saw two grizzly bear cubs playing around the base of a big pine.

"Bears, here?" gasped Kathy.

"That's sure enough what they look like!" replied Bob. "We'd better get past them as fast as we can."

But at that moment the mother bear crashed into view. At sight of the riders she reared to her hind feet and gave a fierce growl. Her jaws yawned open, baring the sharp fangs.

"Have—have we—got—any honey?" stammered Kathy, frightened.

The mother bear suddenly did a curious thing. She turned on the cubs and cuffed them both up the tree.

Linda took advantage of this brief respite to pull an opened box of cookies from her saddlebag. When the grizzly turned on the riders again, growling, she threw the box toward the unfriendly beast. When it hit the ground the cookies spilled out.

The surprised bear, sniffing sweetness, sampled a cookie. Obviously pleased, she went for the others.

Instantly Bob started up and signaled his companions to follow. They rode at a good pace past the bruin, who was still eating voraciously. Not until they came to a wide stream racing over the boulders did the riders slow up, then stop.

Bob glanced around. "This must be Pesky Creek that Cactus Mac mentioned," he said.

They let the horses have a short drink, then went on, eager to get out of the woods. Soon, to their relief, they entered a clearing in which stood a crude cabin. Smoke wafted up from a chimney, and the door was open. Two mongrel dogs, which had been dozing, stood up and barked at the newcomers. A moment later an elderly man appeared in the doorway.

He lifted a hand in greeting and with a broad smile called out, "Halloo!"

"Hi!" called back the foursome, and rode up.

Bob dismounted, introduced himself and the others, explained briefly the purpose of the trail trip, and asked the old man if he would attest on the Trail Blazers' forms to their presence.

"You betcha!" exclaimed the old fellow. "Carl Johnson's my name. Now you just tie your hay burners to some branches and rest a spell while I limber up my writin' pinkies."

The young people grinned at one another and Larry asked, "Do you live here in these woods the year round?"

"That I do," replied Carl Johnson. "I work for the

county watchin' out for fires, and killin' rattlesnakes and coyotes."

"But not bears," Linda declared.

The man gave her a wry smile. "You meet up with a bear?"

Together Linda and Kathy gave a colorful account of their frightening experience with the animals.

Johnson nodded. "That be Jezebel and her cubbies." He shook his head woefully. "Reckon if young people are goin' to start comin' through here, I better go out and git me a bear rug."

"But you can't shoot her now while she's bringing up a family," protested Linda.

Carl Johnson's eyes twinkled. "Didn't exactly aim to do that. I'll just go out and run her back up to the ridge country. Bad fire there this spring drove the bears down."

"But won't she come for you with her awful teeth?" asked Kathy, aghast.

"Not when I point old Pizen there at her." He gestured to his rifle. "Jezebel's gun-shy from havin' been shot at so often—she's had her old hide nicked a time or two."

Linda said, "I didn't know there were bears in this part of California."

"Yup," replied Carl Johnson. "California was overrun with grizzlies at one time. The gay young *caballeros* used to go out with their *reatas* and capture the critters alive so later they could put one in a ring with a savage bull. In the old gold rush days bull-and-bear fights was right popular. 'Tweren't for the lily-livered, but there was them as figgered it was somethin' worth goin' miles to see."

Kathy shuddered. "What gruesome entertainment!" she said with distaste.

"By the way, what is the name of this creek?" Bob asked the woodsman.

"Pescado Creek," he replied.

"That isn't the way Cactus pronounced it." Bob chuckled and his companions laughed at the foreman's calling it Pesky Creek.

"Fish Creek," murmured Linda, translating the Spanish word *pescado*.

After Carl Johnson had signed the attest forms and given them to Linda, he looked at the foursome. "Now," he said, with the corners of his eyes crinkling, "I'll just fry you all up some nice bear steaks."

"Oh no, thanks!" said Kathy quickly, growing pale. "We—we really must be getting along."

The others laughed, realizing that the good-natured old man was joking. Then he said earnestly, "I got me a right fine mess of trout this mornin'. I'd be pleased to have you help me eat 'em. A body gets tired now and then just sittin' down with his dogs."

"But wouldn't we make you short on rations?" said Linda. "How do you get supplies in here?"

Johnson beamed. "Ranger station down the creek a

pace. Fire trail leads to it from the beach highway. Jeep comes up with stuff for the ranger and me."

"Then," said Linda, laughing, "we'd love to eat with you."

The others nodded. "It's past our lunch time anyhow," Bob added. "I'm starved."

While the girls helped Carl Johnson with preparations, the boys loosened the horses' cinches. This done, Larry took several pictures of the cabin and its surroundings.

Johnson soon had a kettle of potatoes boiling in their jackets, the fish cleaned and waiting in clear cold water to be cooked. When everything else was ready, the old woodsman shook the trout in a big sack of corn meal and fried them on a griddle. Everyone declared the fish a treat.

The girls cleaned up after the meal while the boys checked the saddles. Then the foursome mounted, and, calling thanks, waved good-by to their genial host and his tail-wagging dogs.

On the very next rise the riders beheld the Pacific Ocean. "How beautiful!" Kathy exclaimed. "Now that's what I call a welcome sight!"

"And a magnificent one," added Linda admiringly.

"Smell that salt air!" Bob said, sniffing. In the distance they could make out the crescent shore line of Crespi Cove.

According to instructions the foursome was to angle slightly to the north in order to drop down into the cove. They rode out of the pines and into scrub oaks, sycamores, and a tangle of light brush. The soil became loose and silty, causing the horses to slide.

Finally the riders reached the shore of Crespi Cove, a beautiful, hard-packed sandy beach rimmed with slopes. On them grew pink, lavender, and white sand plants in full bloom. From the back wall of one slope trickled a fresh spring.

The four jumped off their horses, ground-hitched them, and stretched.

"Look there!" cried Linda, pointing to a slope against which was anchored a large, sturdy oak frame, heavily glassed. Inside on a plaque was printing.

"That must be the marker," she surmised.

The young people raced over to it and, enthralled, read the inscription:

CRESPI COVE

ON JUNE 1827 THE BLACK-BEARDED PORTUGUESE PIRATE TOMAS SOLA BROUGHT HIS PIRATE SHIP INTO THE SHELTERING HARBOR OF THIS COVE IN ORDER TO ROB THE RICH RANCHOS THAT HAD NO PROTECTING GUNS. WHEN HE CAME ASHORE WITH TWO BLACK BOATMEN IN HIS GIG HE WAS BRAVELY MET BY PADRE SANCHEZ CRESPI OF THE SAN ORTEGO MISSION, WITH A LARGE BURNING CROSS. PADRE CRESPI HAD HIS MISSION IN-

DIANS TIE UP THE PIRATES AND TAKE THEM INTO CAPTIVITY. THE PIRATES WAITING ON THE SHIP WERE TERRIFIED AT SIGHT OF THE FIERY CROSS, AND WHEN THEIR LEADER PIRATE TOMAS DID NOT RETURN THEY SAILED AWAY. THE RANCHOS WERE SAVED FROM THEIR PILLAGE BY THE BRAVE DEED OF PADRE SANCHEZ CRESPI WHOSE NAME THIS COVE BEARS IN HIS HONOR.

Larry took several pictures of the marker from various angles.

By now it was late afternoon, but Linda, turning to look out over the glorious blue Pacific and its foaming surf, exclaimed, "Let's go for a swim!"

The others agreed with enthusiasm and hurried to unsaddle the horses. Each animal was tethered to one of the big rocks on the fringing slope and rubbed down with a piece of gunny sacking. Then the boys shook out the canvas buckets and filled them at the spring. Finally, the horses were given a meal of pellet food.

The Craigs and their friends brought out their bathing suits, which had been carried in the bedrolls. Linda was first to run to the water's edge, and gave a little squeal as the cold water swirled over her feet.

As the next wave came rolling in, she laughed. "Here I go!" she called and dived through it before the wave broke in a high crest of foam. Linda went

under the following wave neatly, then started stroking out in the exhilarating delight of a good swim.

Suddenly she felt something grab one of her ankles. The girl kicked hard to shake it off, but the
grasp grew tighter. It began to pull her under! Frantically Linda wondered if she had been seized by an
octopus or even a shark.

Terror gripped her as she was drawn beneath the
surface, fighting desperately for her life!

VII

A Haughty Rival

In that split moment everything within Linda resisted the idea of perishing underwater. Although her lungs felt as if they were about to burst, the girl's strong instinct for survival forced her to act. She mustered sufficient strength to make a barrel roll in a last hope of twisting free.

As Linda did so, she saw that her assailant was a man, tall and thin, wearing diving equipment, fins, air tank, and mask. Her one quick glance of his face behind the plastic viewplate revealed a small black mustache. He was no one she had ever seen before.

It flashed through the girl's mind that he was merely a sportsman diver amusing himself at her expense. She made a final feeble struggle to break free. Surely he must see that she could not last another minute without air. But the diver did not relinquish his grasp.

Linda felt consciousness ebbing away. At the same

moment she dimly perceived another form dart alongside. Her captor struck out at the newcomer with his free hand. The other swimmer veered, then made a long reach for the diver's mask.

At that, he let go of Linda's ankle and streaked away through the depths. The exhausted girl felt strong arms carrying her upward. As the two broke the surface, Linda saw that her rescuer was Larry.

He kept a supporting arm under her while she slowly took deep, gasping lungsful of air. Finally in a weak voice she said:

"Let's get to shore."

Larry nodded, keeping close as they swam in and rode a breaker onto the smooth beach. Linda snatched off her cap and sank limply to the sand.

Bob and Kathy, greatly worried, knelt by her side. "I—I'll be all right," Linda assured them with a faint smile.

"But what happened?" Kathy cried.

Larry, his face grim, explained.

"Where's the low-down sneak?" Bob exploded. "I'll—"

"I'm afraid he's out of reach by now," said Linda. She turned to Larry and asked, "When did you realize what was happening to me?"

"After I saw you dive through that second wave, I wasn't going to let you swim out any farther alone, so I started after you. I'd almost caught up when you disappeared. It was so sudden I knew something had happened. Believe me, it didn't take me many strokes to find out for sure."

"But who would have been so crazy as to hold you down like that for fun when he knew you couldn't breathe?" asked Kathy, wrapping a towel about Linda.

"I don't think it was for fun," replied Linda, rubbing her bruised ankle.

"One of the Colemans?" Bob speculated. "Out for revenge for our putting the sheriff's men on their track?"

"Not one of the Colemans," said Linda. "This diver was taller, and thin, with a small black mustache."

"It could have been a seagoing confederate of theirs," Kathy suggested.

"Right," Bob agreed. "This is an indication that we are being watched, and our comings and goings are known."

"And it had better be a reminder for us to keep close together and on our guard at all times," Larry warned.

The others solemnly nodded. "No more lone ocean plunges for me," said Linda, laughing. She sat up, declaring she felt fully recovered.

"You know," said Kathy, "with what we've run into, up against, and undergone blazing *this* trail, we ought to qualify for membership in the Royal Order of High Potentates!"

Larry grinned. "And our uniforms should be made of armor plate!"

The increased coolness of the late afternoon made the swimmers shiver. "We'd better get dressed," Kathy advised.

Afterward the boys scooped a hole in the sand and built a small fire. For a few minutes the campers stood stretching cold hands over it and enjoying the warmth.

Presently Bob asked, "What's for supper?"

"Your guess is as good as anybody's," replied Kathy. "What usually comes out of a saddlebag?"

"Beans, bacon, tomatoes," recited Larry. "Jezebel the bear got the cookies."

"You're all wrong." Linda smiled. "We are going to have an appropriate shore dinner—tuna heated in mushroom soup, and toasted English muffins to put it on, and pitted ripe olives. For dessert we'll open some cans of sliced pineapple."

"I'm ready for three helpings!" said Larry.

Suddenly Kathy whispered, "Oh, oh! Looks as if we're going to have company."

The others followed her gaze down the beach and saw a young man in a police uniform approaching. When he reached them, Bob asked, "Are we breaking regulations by building a fire?"

"No. Beach fires are permitted here in the cove," the officer replied pleasantly. "I'm Dick Ferranto of the beach patrol, just making a routine check."

Bob introduced the members of his group, then asked, "Do you know anyone who goes skin diving out here?"

"No one in particular," replied Ferranto. "The frogmen come and go to try out their flippers."

"There's a fellow somewhere out in the ocean who ought to be flipped into your jail," declared Larry. He described the mysterious diver's malicious attack on Linda.

"Very strange," Ferranto commented. "Can you give any kind of personal description?" he asked with keen interest. Linda told what she knew.

"I'll make a report of this to headquarters at once," said Ferranto, "and keep a sharp lookout for the fellow."

He turned his attention to the horses and asked, "Did you folks come far?"

"From San Quinto Valley," replied Linda, and went on to explain the purpose of their trip.

"Breaking a trail across those hills from the far valley will certainly be a great help to both equestrians and hikers," Dick Ferranto said with a smile.

"And this marker at the cove tells a really exciting story," Linda commented.

"There's an interesting sequel to it about Pirate Tomás Sola," said Ferranto.

"You mean that he escaped?" Kathy asked.

"He escaped jail," Ferranto answered, "but not by breaking out. Padre Crespi converted and baptized him. Tom, as he was then called, became one of the most energetic workers of the mission. Before that the habit of *mañana*—wait until tomorrow—was practiced so much among the workers that progress on the buildings had been slow.

"Tom was a powerful man. He hard-bossed a crew, driving them up into the Santa Monica Mountains to fell big trees and broadax them square for use at the mission. Buildings rose in short order. Later Tom Sola constructed some of the finest rancho mansions, and married Magdalena Estrada, a daughter of one of the richest grandees."

"From pirate to prince, eh?" quipped Bob, and the others laughed.

Linda said, "Our Trail Blazers organization has a club in the Malibu. Perhaps you've heard of it."

"I see notices of the club activities in the paper frequently," replied Dick Ferranto. "One of the members is a society girl, and a very fine horsewoman, so her name is often in print. I have become acquainted with her, since she rides here on the beach a lot."

The visitors exchanged meaningful glances and Linda asked casually, "What is her name?"

"Shirley Blaine," replied Ferranto. His face lighted up. "Say! Here she comes now."

The Club 28 representatives looked curiously down the beach and watched the rider approach. She was on a flat saddle, cantering a beautiful chestnut Saddlebred on the hard-packed wet sand. Shirley was a stunning blonde. Linda and Kathy were quick to note also that she wore an expensive tailored turquoise riding habit.

"Hello, Dick," the girl said airily, riding up. She looked at the campers in their jeans and plaid shirts with haughty inquisitiveness.

"Hello, Miss Blaine," returned the officer. "Glad you rode out here this evening. Meet some of your Trail Blazers Club members from the valley." He laughed and added, "Guess you folks had better give your own names."

Linda performed the introductions, mentioning that she and Bob were from Rancho del Sol.

"Oh, from del la Sol," Shirley drawled, with a lift of her eyebrows.

Amused glances passed among the four at her affected and incorrect pronunciation of the ranch's name.

Dick Ferranto said, "Well, I have to continue my rounds," and raised a hand in farewell as he turned away.

Linda addressed Shirley Blaine pleasantly. "We're here on an initiation ride," she told her. "Blazed a trail across the hills. I suppose you went through a similar initiation."

Shirley's pretty face took on a superior look. "Good gracious, no," she exclaimed. "I wouldn't go in for anything like that. I don't care about roughing it. I'm a show ring rider, and my top winning reputation was quite sufficient to qualify me for membership."

Larry gave his friends a wink and said nonchalantly, "Some people have all the luck."

Shirley's eyes narrowed in anger. Quickly Linda said, "I suppose each club makes its own rules for accepting members. Tell me, don't any of yours do trail riding in accordance with the main purpose of the organization?"

"Oh, yes," replied Shirley blithely. "We have a fine chuck wagon in our club for long rides. But I prefer not to trail dust. And I never take care of my own horses. I have a groom for that."

She rode over by the tethered horses, scrutinizing Chica d'Oro appraisingly. Then she asked abruptly of Linda, "This is your filly, isn't she?"

"Why yes," Linda replied, surprised. "Her name is Chica d'Oro. How did you know she belongs to me?"

"Oh, I suppose I've read it in the paper at some time." Shirley continued her critical observation of the palomino. It was evident to the others that she was fascinated. Then to their utter amazement, she asked Linda, "What will you sell her for?"

Linda was certain that Shirley was joking and laughed. "Not for peanuts."

"How much then?" asked Shirley imperiously. "I'd like to buy your horse."

"Chica isn't for sale," said Linda softly.

"Oh, come now," exclaimed Shirley, "everything

has a price. What is Chica d'Oro's? I don't intend to haggle over the cost."

"Chica isn't for sale," repeated Linda with indubitable firmness.

For a few moments marble blue eyes clashed with flashing brown ones.

Anger brought bright spots of color high in Shirley's cheeks. Then she said stiffly, "You may change your mind. When you do, let me know." Without so much as a good-by gesture, she pulled her mount around sharply and cantered off.

"Whew!" Bob whistled. "A real dilly of a spoiled brat! Her Saddlebred is more of a thoroughbred than she is." He made an exaggerated bow before Larry. "She's all yours, buddy boy."

"That's my dust going the other way." Larry grinned broadly.

"It sure gives me duck bumps, Linda," said Kathy worriedly, "to think of you competing against Shirley Blaine in the Trail Blazers big all-clubs show. Why, I wouldn't put it past her to pull any kind of mean trick to win against you."

Linda laughed, but with an inward troubled feeling. "I don't think she'd go that far. If Shirley should try anything unfair in the ring, she'd be disqualified, and what could she do otherwise if I'm careful? Our friend Miss Blaine apparently buys what she wants in this world. But even she can't buy Chica, so that's that!"

Bob was looking thoughtfully at the ocean. "I wonder if she knows that diving hombre?"

"Perhaps," replied Linda. "Although she obviously didn't know we were here, or who we were, until Dick Ferranto introduced us."

"We can't be too sure of that," argued Larry. "Don't forget—*someone* is spying on us."

"I thought you suspected the Colemans, who want revenge for your putting the law on their trail," Kathy said to the Craigs.

"Of course," said Linda. "And I'm positive Shirley isn't mixed up with those thieves!"

Larry changed the subject. "Right now I'd like some chow," he declared.

"Build up the fire again," directed Linda gaily, "and supper will be ready in a jiffy."

With everyone helping, the supper was soon prepared and served. After eating, the four relaxed and watched the rising moon strike a silvery path across the water.

Larry gave a low chuckle. "This reminds me of another fish dinner I've heard about."

"Give!" Kathy laughed and they all settled back to listen to one of Larry's good yarns.

"This happened up on 'the river of no return,' the Salmon River in central Idaho," he began. "A bunch of cowboys were working across the hill flushing the new calves out of the brush for branding. They'd had a hard time. It had rained some, the brush was thick, and the cows were their usual ornery selves keeping hidden. Already the crew had been out two days longer than expected. Their clothes were damp, their skin itched, and their stomachs were rebelling against Dutch-oven stew and biscuits.

"With at least two more days of work ahead of them, the trail boss called in two men, Windy and Frankie, and told them to go over to the river and catch a couple of big salmon, and not to fail.

"Happy at this respite, the two cowboys rigged up a couple of lines and rode their horses to the river. Frankie worried for fear they wouldn't be able to catch a salmon, but Windy assured him they could probably pull out a couple with their bare hands.

"At the river the cowboys baited their hooks with fat grubs they found in the shore dirt. They fished and fished without so much as getting a nibble.

"Windy concluded that they would have to find better bait, and they started looking for it. Well, Windy ran across a big black snake with a frog in its mouth.

"He grabbed the snake and eased the frog out. Then at the reproachful look in the snake's eyes at stealing its dinner, Windy took a bottle of cough syrup from his hip pocket and poured a long drink down the snake's throat. The reptile rolled and writhed in delighted appreciation. Windy then baited his hook with the frog and immediately pulled in a big salmon.

"He and Frankie hunted for another frog, but were unable to find one. As the day wore on, Windy went back to his grub bait while Frankie kept hunting for something better. They knew one salmon wouldn't be enough for all the boys at the cow camp, and that the two who would go without would be—Windy and Frankie. Besides, they'd likely get a chapping! They felt pretty low.

"All of a sudden, Windy became aware of a tugging on his jean leg. Thinking he had snagged it on a root, he reached down to loosen himself. And there was that big old black snake holding up another frog!"

As Larry finished his story, the others burst into laughter and Bob gave a mock groan. "For a tall tale like that—throw him in the ocean!"

At this Larry pulled off his boots and dived into his sleeping bag. "No thanks!" he called out. "I've had my ducking for the day."

Bob yawned. "I'm going to hit the sack myself."

"Best idea yet!" Linda agreed sleepily.

The bedrolls had been arranged in a crescent around the horses so that any of the four could instantly hear the slightest suspicious sound.

Within minutes after "good nights" were exchanged, everyone fell asleep. Linda was suddenly awakened by the bright beam of a flashlight full in her face. As she sat up with a little cry, the girl saw a figure slipping cautiously away. She hastily pulled on her boots and ran to awaken Bob.

"A man had a light on me," Linda whispered. "I see him out there. Let's try to catch him!"

Bob had his boots on by the time Linda had finished speaking and together they raced after the skulking shape of the mysterious intruder.

VIII

Timber!

As the Craigs raced after the intruder they saw him scramble up the embankment and head for the rugged back country.

Suddenly Linda exclaimed, "There's someone else!" She pointed to the figure of another man who had raced from the opposite direction and was running after the first. "The Coleman brothers, I'll bet!" she added with a gasp.

"If we could only get a glimpse of their faces to be sure!" said Bob.

Then the second man shone his flashlight on the back of the other.

"That one seems thinner than either of the Colemans," remarked Linda as she climbed breathlessly.

"Maybe he's the diver," Bob suggested.

The first man, who had a good head start, was suddenly swallowed up by the dense underbrush into which he had run. Linda and Bob stopped, knowing it was useless, in the darkness, to continue their pursuit over the rugged terrain. The man with the light stopped also. Then he turned and approached the Craigs.

Linda shuddered a little as the tall, thin figure drew closer. Bob stood with knotted fists, ready to fend off any attack. In a few moments, they recognized the man as beach patrol Officer Dick Ferranto!

Relieved but surprised, Linda asked him, "Was it you who shone the light on me?"

"Yes," Ferranto admitted. "I decided to make a quick survey to satisfy myself that everything was all right. I spotted that fellow sneaking up to your camp. Unfortunately he heard my approach and slipped back into the shadows. That's when I shone my light on you to see if he had done any of you harm. Then I hurried away and tried cutting him off. But he had the jump on me."

"Did you get a look at his face?" asked Bob.

"No, I didn't," replied Ferranto. "He kept his face ducked down as he ran. But he seems to be a tall, wiry fellow—he may be the diver who held your sister underwater."

"That's what I suspect," Bob remarked. "Any news on that nut's identity?"

"Not so far," Ferranto answered. "Files are being checked, and a lead may come in tomorrow."

The three had walked back to the camp as they talked. Kathy and Larry, awakened by the sudden commotion, were standing with their boots on, waiting anxiously.

"What happened?" Kathy demanded.

"We had an intruder snooping around," Linda explained. "Officer Ferranto was checking here when he spotted the man. We all chased him—but no luck."

"Which one of our mysterious enemies do you think he is?" Kathy asked, looking about her nervously.

Ferranto smiled. "Don't let this keep you folks awake," he said. "The fellow may have been just a beachcomber hunting for food or anything else of value he could pick up."

"It's a possibility," Larry remarked, but without conviction.

"Can you manage all right if I go down the beach for a while?" Ferranto asked.

"Yes," Bob replied. "We're used to looking out for ourselves."

"A million thanks for your help," Linda spoke up.

"All in the line of duty," the young officer said. "Good night, and sleep well." He went on his way.

The horses meanwhile had become restive at the fracas, and were pawing the ground and blowing through their nostrils. Linda hurried to Chica d'Oro, stroked her neck, and talked softly until the filly calmed down. This had a soothing effect on the other animals.

"It looks as if someone is out to trip us up," Linda

murmured to the palomino. "But baby, we're sticking together, and the troublemakers will find us a hard pair to beat!"

Chica nickered softly as she was accustomed to doing when Linda talked to her. The girl returned to her companions. After discussing the mysterious man awhile, Kathy said, "Well, boots off, everyone, and back into the bags!"

"You all get some sleep," Larry urged. "I'm standing watch until daybreak."

"I'll spell you," Bob offered.

"I'll crawl in," said Linda, "but I know I won't be able to sleep."

Kathy yawned. "I will. But one good yell from Larry or Bob, and I'll come up fighting."

Despite Linda's prediction, exhaustion took its toll, and she dropped off to sleep. When she awoke it was morning. The boys stood by a little cook fire that they had just finished building.

Kathy still slept soundly, her features tranquil. Impishly Linda picked up a tiny pebble and tossed it onto her friend's forehead. Kathy's eyes flew open and darted around, taking in the peaceful scene. Then she murmured, "Mm," and closed her lids again.

"No, you don't!" Linda laughed, crawled out, and shook Kathy's bag. "Up you go!" she said.

"Come on, you two cooks," called Bob. "Fire's ready and we're weak from hunger."

"Did you boys get any sleep?" asked Linda solicitously.

"We both got some—enough," Bob replied.

Kathy had emerged from her sleeping bag. She stretched, flung out her arms, and whirled in a gay pivot on the table-top hard sand. "What a gorgeous morning!" she sang. It was a bright one, the ocean scintillating under the burnished gold of the sun.

"It makes everything that happened last night seem like only a bad dream," Linda mused.

"But definitely not to be forgotten," cautioned Bob.

"Right," said Larry, "until we have our hands on a certain tall, thin fellow, and he has answered a few questions."

While the girls prepared breakfast, the boys watered and fed the horses. In a short while the campers were enjoying crisp bacon, toasted muffins, and a pot of steaming fragrant cocoa.

"After this meal, I'm ready to take on a whole gang of intruders," declared Bob, grinning.

"They're all yours!" Kathy retorted promptly.

When the four had finished eating, they began packing up their gear for the trip home. Linda, suddenly grinning mischievously, jumped on Chica bareback, and raced her toward the surf. As a big wave broke and the foaming water rolled toward the filly, she stopped so abruptly that Linda nearly went over her head. Chica backed almost as rapidly as she had gone forward.

Linda leaned down and said soothingly, "Okay, baby, I guess you don't want an ocean dip, but you nearly gave me one!"

Everyone laughed and felt in good spirits to start their long ride home. They saddled, fastened on the equipment, and were ready to set out when Dick Ferranto appeared.

"Glad to see you're safe and well this morning," he said.

"We're fine thanks," Linda replied gaily. "*Hasta la vista.*" She smiled as they waved to the officer and rode off.

They had no trouble finding the trail, since Bob had left one of his tape markers on a sycamore at the point where they had emerged onto Crespi Cove.

It was cool beneath the shade of the thickly-leaved branches of the trees. Kathy shivered and said, "I wish I had remembered to bring along some of that beach sunshine."

"Maybe we'll meet a nice warm bear," Larry teased.

Linda had been scrutinizing the ground as they rode along. Now she said, "I'm sure I see prints on this trail besides those made by our horses. Do you suppose other riders are making use of it already?"

"I hope it isn't one of our enemies!" Kathy exclaimed.

"If that is the case," Linda said, frowning, "he's ahead of us."

"Lying in wait, no doubt," concluded Kathy nervously.

Bob and Larry studied the unfamiliar horseshoe marks more closely.

"There's been one other horse along here all right," Larry declared.

"Let's not borrow trouble," Linda advised. "But we'd better be on our guard just the same."

A little distance farther along she and the others were forced to rein in. A huge fallen tree lay across their path, with great upreaching branches house-high. The tree lay in a spot where the underbrush was extremely dense. Everyone stared in awe at the tremendous trunk.

"There must have been a fury of a gale up here to blow this giant down," Linda remarked.

"But there's no other indication of a strong wind," Larry pointed out. "No broken branches lying around, or any heavy scatter of leaves."

"What could have caused the tree to fall?" asked Linda, puzzled. "It looks healthy, not rotted inside."

"It couldn't have been pushed," said Kathy wryly.

"With the help of a good stout ax or saw it could have crashed," Bob speculated.

"What a shame—to cut down such a beautiful big old tree!" Linda sighed. "Why?"

"I don't know," Bob replied. "But I guess we'll have to start cutting our way through the brush around it at one end or the other if it takes all day."

"I think we might do a quicker job by hacking the branches in the middle," Linda suggested. "Then we can jump the horses over."

"Right," said Larry. "Let's get at it."

The foursome dismounted, ground-hitched their horses, and went to work on the branches. The boys used their bowie knives on the limbs, while the girls broke away the smaller ones by hand. When they finally had cleared the section of trunk lying across the trail, the obstacle was only about two feet high.

"Go ahead, Linda," said Bob. "Chica's the best jumper. She'll be a good example for the others."

Linda lifted her palomino easily over the trunk.

"You next, Kathy," Larry said.

"I don't think so," demurred Kathy. "Patches doesn't see any sense in jumping unless there's a good reason. If the other horses are on the far side, then she'll want to follow them."

"Check," Larry agreed, and put Jubilee over the trunk.

Bob followed. Jubilee and Rocket did not execute the jump with the grace that Chica had, but, being well-trained trail horses, getting over an obstruction was all in a day's work for them.

Kathy then took Patches back a few paces for a run at the jump. Instead of taking it, the mare stopped suddenly. Kathy went flying over her head into broken-off branches on the other side of the tree.

She lay motionless.

"Oh!" Linda cried out fearfully.

Instantly she and the boys were off their horses and on their knees beside the fallen rider.

"Kathy! Kathy!" exclaimed Linda, taking her friend's limp hand. "Bob, hand me a canteen."

He quickly unscrewed the top of one and Linda soaked her yellow cotton neckerchief with the cool water, which she swabbed over Kathy's face.

The girl opened her eyes and sat up. "Ooooh," she groaned. "Did I—ever get the—wind knocked out of me!"

Bob asked anxiously, "Are you sure you're all right otherwise?"

"Sure," Kathy insisted.

"Well, you just lie back quietly for a few minutes until you feel a little steadier," Linda admonished.

Surprisingly, Kathy did so without argument. Worried glances were exchanged among the others. On the opposite side of the tree trunk, Patches was nosing unconcernedly at the edge of the path for any tasty morsel that she might find.

"I'll bring that balky pony over in a hurry when we're ready to go on," said Bob. "Right now I think I'll investigate the base of this tree and see if it was felled." He pushed his way through the brush.

Linda meanwhile began to examine more closely the mysterious horseshoe prints. "They're smaller than those of our four horses," she commented. "But they don't go any farther on the trail. Right here the prints turn off into the woods."

Bob returned. Grimly he informed them, "The tree was felled all right."

Linda gave him a meaningful look. "Do you think it was done to stop *us?*" she asked.

"That's my hunch," her brother replied.

"Mine, too," Larry added.

Kathy raised herself up on one elbow. "Why would anyone go to so much trouble?" she wondered in alarm.

"And why would he want to block our path here?" Linda puzzled.

No one had an answer. "Trying to solve this riddle now isn't going to get us anywhere," said Bob finally. "We'd better keep close together. We may have company nearby."

Kathy shuddered and said in a low tone, "I almost feel as if eyes were peering out at me from the brush."

Larry frowned. "Whoever cut down this tree obviously will go to great lengths to hamper us."

"What, actually, could he hope to gain by it?" Linda countered. "Except to delay us awhile, which is no great harm."

"I have a feeling it's an ambush," Kathy spoke up.

Bob tried to sound reassuring. "I didn't see a sign of anyone back there in the brush. Have any of you heard a suspicious noise?"

The others shook their heads.

"Evidently the tree feller was alone," Bob went on. "He must have iron muscles."

"Like those of a swimmer, for instance?" asked Linda, and glanced down at her ankle. "An underwater swimmer? The one who grabbed me surely had fingers like a vise and could wield an ax powerfully."

"Yes," said Larry, "and he could also be the prowler in our camp. But *who* is he, and what grudge has he against us?"

"I'm sure," Linda replied, "that the grudge is against Chica d'Oro and me. It makes me feel bad that the rest of you have to be involved."

"What do you mean?" said Larry. "We thrive on it!"

Bob clenched a fist. "One of these days that sneak is going to get caught, and then he'll do some talking!"

At that moment Bob happened to look at Kathy, who had grown very pale. "How do you feel?"

"Like getting out of here," she replied, and Bob helped the girl to her feet.

"Everybody mount up," he said. "Kathy, you get aboard Rocket, then all of you start ahead slowly."

Bob now leaped back over the fallen tree, pulled Patches' head up, and wound her reins around the saddle horn. Her attention was caught by the departing horses, and she whinnied but did not budge.

"Guess I'll have to try stronger methods," said Bob. He dismounted, cut a small green switch from a bush, gave a war whoop, and brought the switch down across Patches' rump.

The mare leaped and fairly flew over the trunk. "Like Pegasus, the flying horse," thought Bob, grinning. He scrambled over the tree trunk himself, helped Kathy onto Patches, and mounted Rocket.

The group rode along quietly, keeping alert eyes to each side. Except for a few birds rustling overhead in the branches, there was not a sound. When they came to the spot where the trail met Pescado Creek, the sun was directly overhead.

"How about stopping here for lunch?" Linda proposed.

There was unanimous assent. The riders loosened the saddle cinches and slipped off the bridles so the horses could drink and do a little grazing. Linda brought out some cans of spiced meat, pumpernickel bread, and apples.

Kathy slumped down on the mossy ground with a sigh. "Count me out. I feel a little too squeamish to eat." She smiled, but her companions noted with concern that she was still white. The weary girl lay back and, as the others ate, went to sleep.

"It might be more than squeamishness," said Larry softly. "Perhaps Kathy's suffered some injury."

"If so, we'd better get a jeep to take her out," Linda whispered.

"I doubt that even a jeep could make it on this narrow trail," replied Larry.

"If Kathy doesn't feel better," murmured Bob, "we'll both ride on Rocket, and go to that ranger station Carl Johnson mentioned. A jeep stops there."

Linda took Kathy's pulse and, lifting a worried face, announced, "It's weak. I don't think we'd better move her yet."

The boys agreed, and the three began a long, tense vigil while trying to decide on the best thing to do.

IX

Prisoners of the Sand

The next few hours were anxious ones for Linda and the boys. They had decided to let Kathy sleep, and at last were relieved to note color returning to her face.

Again Linda checked her friend's pulse. "It's stronger," she announced thankfully.

Just then Kathy stirred and stretched her arms over her head.

Bob said, "Hello, Sleeping Beauty."

She opened one blue eye and winked at him. "It's an unlucky trail bunch that doesn't have one," she retorted. Then Kathy sat up. "I feel fine—except for a certain ache in my middle from hunger. Anyone save me a crumb?"

The others laughed, exchanging looks of relief. Linda hastily spread potted meat on some slices of pumpernickel. Bob brought a cup of clear cold creek water. Larry handed Kathy an apple.

"Anything more weird happen since I saw you last?" she asked.

"Not a thing," Linda assured her.

"We're slipping." Kathy grinned.

As she ate Bob proposed his plan to take her to the Ranger Station for a jeep ride out to the valley.

"What kind of a Trail Blazer would that make me?" Kathy objected. "Thanks, but I'm back in the saddle and rarin' to ride. Honest."

"Good. Let's go!" said Bob.

They mounted and continued their leisurely pace along the trail. The young people found the fragrance of the pines and the music of the babbling creek enchanting.

"Looks as if our guardian angel has caught up with us." Kathy sighed with pleasure.

"We'd better enjoy all this while we can," remarked Larry.

"You mean, this is the calm before the storm?" asked Kathy.

"I'm no prophet." Larry grinned.

"A horseback philosopher, then?" Linda smiled.

"I haven't decided." Larry chuckled. "But I'll let you know."

When they reached Carl Johnson's cabin, Linda exclaimed at once, "Look there! A lot of fresh horseshoe prints since those we made early yesterday."

"Riders *are* using our trail already," said Bob.

"Well, three cheers for us," said Kathy gaily. "At

least we got it cut through and marked. Nobody seemed to want to stop us from doing that."

Just then old Carl came running from the cabin gripping his rifle. On recognizing his callers he immediately dropped it down and exclaimed, "By cracky! You're a right welcome sight to these old eyes."

The four dismounted and Linda said, "I see that you've had other horseback visitors already."

"Humph!" Carl grunted. "Visitors you be a-callin' 'em! Varmints, that's what they was. They cleaned me out of all my vittles."

"How many were there, and what did they look like?" asked Linda with quick interest.

"Two of 'em there was," growled Carl, "and a rough-lookin' pair. Both had dark hair and mean dark eyes, and weren't shaved. One was short and stocky, and had a flat broad nose. Ugly, he was. The other fellow was nearer to medium height, and took orders from the squat hombre."

"They're probably hiding out if they had to steal food," Larry deduced.

"Could be," replied Carl. "They was mighty concerned as to who made this new trail. Worried, I reckon, that they'd ridden smack into lawman territory. When I told 'em it was blazed by some young folks from the valley, they didn't appear any better pleased."

"It could have been those petty cattle rustlers,"

106

said Linda excitedly. "They've probably heard that members of our club are helping the posse to track them down."

"What sort of horses were the men riding?" asked Bob.

"The critters was rough-lookin' too," replied Carl. "Just a couple of jugheady, long-haired brownies."

"Let's search for clues," Linda urged. "Do you mind if we take a peek inside?" she asked the cabin owner.

"Course not," said Carl. "Them two thievin' crooks didn't bother to ask. Just barged in and cleaned me out, they did. Even took my flour."

"We don't have much food left," said Linda, "but we'll leave you what we have."

"Don't you be a-shortin' yourselves," Carl protested. "Soon as the sun gits a little lower, I'll wade down-creek and get me a nice mess of trout. Come mornin', I'll foot it to the Ranger Station and pick up supplies."

"We won't need the food," Linda insisted. "We'll be home by dinnertime."

She and her friends went through the saddlebags and gave Johnson the rest of the pumpernickel, a can of meat, half a pound of bacon, and several apples.

"Thanks, this'll tide me over," he said.

"Where are your dogs?" Kathy inquired wonderingly.

"I set 'em a-chasin' Jezebel and her cubbies back into the high country."

"Won't they get lost?" Kathy asked.

Old Carl chuckled. "Not those two. They'll be back when they get good 'n' ready. No need to worry. They always come back, fat and full of ginger, the rascals."

"Couldn't you have run those two thieves off with your rifle?" asked Larry.

Old Carl shook his head, scowling, and replied, "Worst luck, I'd left Pizen—my rifle—standin' up against a tree out back after I'd come from the bear chasin'. When I seen that short ruffian had a revolver pushed through his belt under his coat, I figured a few vittles wasn't worth arguin' over."

"Did you hear one call the other by name?" Bob queried.

"Nope," replied Carl. "That ugly-nosed punk jest called t'other, 'Hey, you,' with him only answerin' by bobbin' his head up and down."

"Which way did they go from here?" asked Linda.

"They cut off there to the side of the cabin," Carl told her. "Said they'd better get off the trail."

The Craigs exchanged excited glances with their friends. "They surely could be the rustlers," said Linda. "Whoever they are, they're armed and dangerous. We have a good description of them and that information ought to help the authorities catch them."

The young people looked inside the cabin and

around the clearing for any further clues but found none.

"It's too bad we aren't equipped to lift finger-prints," said Linda. "There must be dozens all over the cabin."

She brought the attest papers inside from her saddle pouch. Once again Carl Johnson affixed his signature to them.

"Will you be riding back through here another day?" he asked a bit wistfully.

"I'm sure we will," replied Bob. "And many of our other friends also."

"Now that will be right nice." Old Carl beamed. "A body gets a mite lonesome at times, especially when his doggies are a-traipsin'."

Linda noticed that Kathy sat at the table with her head in her hands. "Do you feel all right?" she asked gently.

"Of course," Kathy replied quickly.

"You look pretty pale again," said Bob. "Maybe this ride back is too hard for you after your spill."

"Think nothing of it," said Kathy with a forced grin. "A few hours of sun-bathing will fix me up."

Her nonchalance did not fool Linda, who realized her friend should have medical attention. In a few minutes the group mounted, waved good-by to Carl Johnson, and continued along the trail.

"At least we needn't worry about meeting Jezebel and her cubs." Bob laughed.

"That's lucky," said Kathy, "since we don't have even a cooky crumb to toss her."

When they arrived at the gasoline station, the riders found that the young mechanic had almost completed the repair work on Chica's trailer. While they waited, Linda noted with concern that Kathy appeared paler than ever and exchanged knowing glances with the others. They must get Kathy home as rapidly as possible!

"I suggest," said Bob, "that we cut off the freeway through Manzanita Canyon and take the desert road past the old borax works to Valley Boulevard, which is just about a mile from your house, Kathy."

"You'll do no such thing," protested Kathy with a spurt of spirit. "That'll make you all late getting home. I'll ride back the same way I came to del Sol."

Linda said with forced cheerfulness, "But I'm sure the route Bob has suggested will be the nicest. I love that drive through Manzanita Canyon."

"Settled," declared Larry.

Kathy gave them a reproachful look, then sighed. "Guess I can't overrule the majority."

A short while later the mechanic announced that the trailer was ready. The travelers stored their gear in the cars and loaded the horses. To Linda's relief Chica walked in without objecting, her scare forgotten.

At Kathy's insistence, the foursome stopped at

Scotty's Steak House for a snack. "You all must be starved," she said.

Linda and the boys ordered apple pie and milk. Kathy herself, however, who sometimes would get up in the middle of the night to eat a piece of pie, had only a few sips of milk. Again her friends exchanged looks of concern.

"Let's go!" Linda urged.

Outside once more, Bob pushed the gear, which was in the station wagon, to one side and unrolled a sleeping bag. "Into the sack," he commanded Kathy.

She began to object but finally shrugged with a wry smile, saying, "Honestly, I do think it will feel good to flop down."

The caravan moved at a moderate pace through Manzanita Canyon, which took its name from the red-limbed manzanita bushes banking the sides of the road. They were abloom with clusters of tiny, pinkish-white, bell-like blossoms. Above the riders here and there appeared the larger wild cherry bushes with their glossy spiny leaves and big bright red berries, which Californians use in making wreaths at Christmas time.

Bob watched keenly for the short cut desert road. He was relieved to find that it was still marked by a dilapidated sign at its entrance bearing the name of the borax works.

This part of the trip proved to be dreary going. On all sides as far as one could see were stretches of sand, broken only by scattered dry scrub brush. From behind it a jack rabbit hopped occasionally.

After a while the travelers came to an apparently newly erected detour sign. They knew it was recent because paint deteriorates quickly in the hot desert air, but on this sign it was fresh and bright.

Bob stopped and came back to Larry's car. "There must have been a washout on the road ahead," he guessed.

Linda said, "Probably a cloudburst cut a deep arroyo."

"We don't have any choice but to follow the detour road," said Larry.

Linda had gone forward to speak to Kathy. The blond girl was sleeping again, but not peacefully. She was moving restlessly, and her face held an expression of pain.

Hurrying to the boys, Linda said worriedly, "We'd better get Kathy home just as soon as possible. She doesn't look well."

Bob nodded and cautioned Larry, "We'll have to take it carefully. This detour isn't more than a wide path in the sand. It doesn't appear to be used much, except by the road crew." He pointed to jeep tire tracks in the sand.

"Probably not," said Linda, "since the borax works haven't been operating for years. The road is kept open by the county because it's cross-country."

Bob returned to the del Sol station wagon and

slowly turned it into the detour. The sand was loose and deep—evidently no attempt had been made to pack it down. But by maintaining a steady, slow pace, the two cars managed to keep rolling and covered a good distance.

Suddenly the station wagon wheels commenced to spin. Instantly Bob shut off the engine. He jumped out and looked ahead.

Linda and Larry hastily joined him. "I'm stuck too," Larry stated in disgust.

Bob's face was grim. "This was no detour," he declared angrily. "The other tire marks end here. The jeep that made them apparently turned back at this spot. No wonder that detour sign looks new. It was put there on purpose so we'd get stuck in this sand!"

"Oh, how dreadful! And with Kathy so sick!" Linda cried out in despair. "But who would have known we were coming this way? We didn't decide to until we were at the service station."

Larry's eyes narrowed. "Wait a minute!" he exclaimed. "I noticed a fellow standing near our outfits at the garage. He seemed to be looking them over with interest. I thought at the time he was waiting to have his car serviced."

"But actually," Linda put in, "he may have been planning a way to stop us."

"Exactly," Bob agreed. "He easily could have overheard our plans to take the short cut."

"What does the man look like?" Linda queried.

Larry frowned in concentration. "I hardly noticed. I do remember that he wore an open-throat T-shirt, had a hairy chest, and muscular arms."

"Strong enough to cut down a tree by himself?" said Bob pointedly.

"I'm sure of it," replied Larry. "But why all these efforts to delay us?" he asked in complete bafflement.

A frightening thought widened Linda's eyes. "Do you suppose it was to keep us away from Rancho del Sol so the Colemans and Trask could ransack the house again?"

Bob shook his head. "I doubt that. They must know by this time that Bronco has armed guards on the place."

"I hope so," said Linda. "Right now we must get out of this predicament. But how?"

"A good-sized tractor would come in handy," said Larry dryly. "Maybe one of us should start walking and try to find help."

"Nobody could stand walking far in this heat," Bob objected, wiping his face with his handkerchief, "not even a horse. There's something else we can try first. It's a trick I saw a sergeant do years ago when our dad was stationed in the Imperial Valley."

"What was it?" asked Larry hopefully.

"Let most of the air out of the tires to get traction," Bob explained, "but leave enough in to get us to a gas station."

He and Larry set about the task immediately.

While they worked, Linda checked again on Kathy. Her face was slightly moist from the heat. Linda opened all the car windows for maximum circulation.

After the boys had finished their job, Bob said, "The horses will have to be taken out to lighten the load as much as possible, and led to the main road. We'll take Rocket and Jubilee out first and ground-hitch them. Linda, you hold Chica and Patches."

When the horses had been removed from the trailers, Bob and Larry started the cars. The deflated tires enabled the boys to move the vehicles inch by inch from the sand.

In the meantime Linda had caught up the tie ropes of the black and bay and, with two horses on each side, started walking. The intense heat soon made her head feel as though it was about to burst.

Bob pulled up alongside her and jumped out. "You drive now and I'll walk."

"Thanks," Linda said gratefully.

Presently they came to the detour marker. Bob laid out a blanket and pulling up the freshly painted sign, carefully wrapped it. "There might be plenty of fingerprints on this," he declared.

When the group finally reached the Highway House, Mrs. Hamilton ran out and smilingly greeted them. "Welcome home, nomads!" But immediately the slim, sweet-faced woman sobered and asked, "Where's Kathy?"

"Sleeping," replied Linda, and explained about the accident.

"Is—is she badly hurt?" gasped Mrs. Hamilton.

"There are no broken bones," Linda assured her.

Mrs. Hamilton hurried to the car and opened the door. "Kathy," she called softly. "Kathy."

The girl opened her eyes. "Mother!" she said groggily. "How did you get here?"

"You're home." Bob laughed.

"Home already!" Kathy sat up suddenly. "And without anything else happening to us!"

Her three friends looked at one another but decided against relating what had happened in the desert. Kathy scrambled out. The next instant her knees started to buckle.

Bob caught her and said to Larry, "Chair service."

They clasped their hands together to make a seat and carried the girl inside the house to her room. Kathy's mother and Linda followed.

"Please call Dr. Kelly to come right out," Mrs. Hamilton requested Linda, "while I help Kathy into bed."

The physician arrived shortly. In a little while he gave his report on Kathy to the tense group.

"She's suffering from shock," he said. "It's nothing that a week in bed and the proper medicine won't fix. There's no cause for worry," he added. "Kathy's sleeping now." Everyone drew a sigh of relief.

As soon as the doctor had left, Mrs. Hamilton

turned to the Craigs. "My goodness!" she exclaimed. "I was so upset I forgot to tell you Craigs that your grandmother called. She expected you home earlier and thought perhaps you had stopped here to visit. She said someone had phoned from the Trail Blazers head office in Los Angeles that all attest papers must be in their hands by six o'clock this evening or the entries won't be valid. You'd have to wait another year before being granted membership."

Bob took a quick look at his watch. "It's five minutes to six now," he groaned.

Linda and the boys stared at one another, aghast.

"We've lost out!" Linda cried dejectedly. "We'll have to disqualify ourselves!"

X

Surprising News

It was a somber trio that pulled into Rancho del Sol and entered the house.

They were warmly welcomed by Mr. and Mrs. Mallory, but Dona's face was deeply troubled. "I am so sorry you didn't get your attest papers into the Los Angeles office before the deadline," she said at once.

"A tough break," Bronco sympathized.

For a minute there was glum silence. Linda broke it by saying, "It does seem peculiar that such a sudden, last-minute notice would be given us by what seems to be a friendly, square-shooting local group."

"It *is* odd, all right," Bob agreed.

Linda turned to her grandmother. "Dona," she said, "could you tell us what the person sounded like who phoned, and the gist of the message?"

"I believe so." Mrs. Mallory looked thoughtful. "I remember thinking at the time that the young woman

118

who called sounded rather giddy to be holding a responsible position at the head office of the organization."

"Why was that, Mrs. Mallory?" asked Larry.

"Because she didn't sound at all businesslike," Dona replied disapprovingly. "When I told her the Craigs were not at home, the woman announced melodramatically that your attest papers would simply *have* to be in the head office by six o'clock, or you would not qualify for membership in the Number 28 Club.

"Then, obviously curious, she asked me where you were, Linda and Bob. When I told her you had not returned from the initiation ride, I distinctly heard her give a little laugh. Although," Dona continued, "the very next second she went on in a gushing fashion to say that all the members would be so sorry not to have you join the Trail Blazers this year."

Larry and Bob paced back and forth angrily. "What creepy luck!" Larry fumed.

Linda had remained in deep thought during her grandmother's recital. Now she looked at the others speculatively. "You know, I have a feeling that woman's sympathy was put on. Furthermore, I'm sure the Trail Blazers office closes at five o'clock, so why would she have said six?"

"Right," Bob put in. "Besides, I never heard of any deadline regulation for our attest papers."

"Same here," Larry stated.

"That settles it," Linda said determinedly. "I'm going to phone Los Angeles. Someone may still be at the Trail Blazers office and can tell me if this whole thing is correct, or just some kind of a practical joke or hoax."

"Good idea," Bob agreed. "While you're calling, Larry and I will take care of the horses and store the gear in the tack room."

Linda's call to the head office met with no response. Next, she hunted up the home number of their secretary, and phoned. She received no answer there either.

Linda then called Sue Mason, the secretary of Club 28. Sue said she had never heard of the regulation. "It might be a new one, though, that our club hasn't been advised about. Linda," she said, "Chuck Eller is on his way over here. You'd better talk to him. I'll have him call you."

As Linda hung up, Bob and Larry came into the hall. "Find out anything?" Bob asked her eagerly.

As Linda shook her head, the phone rang and she hurriedly answered. "Oh, hi, Chuck!" Linda told him the message Dona had received. For a moment there was absolute silence on Chuck's end of the wire. Then he exploded:

"What! Ridiculous! You bet that call was a fake!"

When Linda hung up the phone her eyes were shining. "It was a hoax," she cried joyously. "Boys, we can get our papers and pics in any time. But the first rustler-tracking ride will take place in a few days, and the next week the big All Clubs convene will be held. So we'd better get our qualifications down to Los Angeles—fast!"

Bob let out his special brand of war whoop, and said, "I'll deliver the papers first thing tomorrow morning."

"That's terrific news!" Larry exclaimed. "I'll take the films home and develop them tonight. Bob, stop by for the prints on your way to Los Angeles tomorrow."

Happily Linda turned back to the phone. "I'll call Mrs. Hamilton and ask her to pass the good word along to Kathy." As she finished the call, Linda gave a hungry sniff. "Mm! One of Luisa's special hams with spices. And am I starved!"

Larry grinned. "I'm glad you invited me to dinner."

The three rushed into the kitchen where Luisa stood watching over her food-laden stove.

"When do we eat?" Bob asked.

"*O mio, mio,*" gasped Luisa. "It is ready, waiting and waiting. I will bring the dinner in to the table quick."

"I'll help you," Linda offered.

In the dining room, the young people brought Bronco and Dona up to date on the events of the trail-blazing ride. The Mallorys expressed great concern at the thought that someone was obviously bent on harming the young initiates, especially Linda, and her horse Chica.

"What possible motive could anyone have for doing such dreadful things!" Dona exclaimed, while her husband's face tightened in anger.

"Whatever it is," Bronco said, "I'm keeping the guard here day and night until we find out and the men responsible are captured."

Dona looked at Linda and Bob in alarm. "I am worried about your leaving here on trips," she stated.

"I promise not to go alone," said Linda. "But we must help to catch those rustlers if we expect to be good Trail Blazers."

Bob looked perplexed. "Our enemies must have another reason besides the Perez jewels for trying to annoy and even harm us. That phony call about the attest papers, for instance—I can't imagine the Coleman gang having anything to gain by that. Why would *they* want to keep us out of the Trail Blazers Club?"

"I hate to say this," Larry put in, "but it looks as though you might have two different groups to contend with."

Luisa came in to serve dessert. Noticing the troubled expressions of those at the table, she attempted to divert them.

"Do not forget tomorrow," the housekeeper said. "It is the day of the big Santa Clarita Guild Fair—and we take my chili vinegar."

Bob regretfully explained that his trip to Los Angeles the following morning would prevent his accompanying the group.

Bronco too would be busy. "I'm sorry I can't drive you to the fair grounds," he said. "But I guess you three ladies can manage."

His wife smiled. "I am sure we can."

Presently Larry went off in his car. Next morning Bob drove away in the pickup, leaving the station wagon for the transportation of the chili vinegar. He had with him the attest papers on which the new trail had been plainly mapped. This would be substantiated by the pictures taken en route, including the marker at Crespi Cove. Bob would stop at Larry's to pick them up.

Meanwhile Linda had found the kitchen a bustle of activity. The usual orderliness of the room was transformed into a jumble of bottles and packing cases. Luisa, who had filled the bottles the night before, was attempting to affix the Rancho del Sol labels which Dona had printed.

This was the housekeeper's big day and she was excited and nervous. The labels either landed on the bottles crooked or would not stick. Luisa threw up her hands with a volley of exclamations in her native tongue.

Linda smiled. "I'll put the labels on," she offered, "while you start filling the boxes."

Finally everything was ready, and the cases

packed into the station wagon. Everyone hurried off to dress. Luisa put on a colorful native Mexican dress. Dona and Linda wore white eyelet embroidery-trimmed Spanish fiesta blouses, and stuck red roses in their dark hair.

Dona seated herself beside Linda, who took the wheel. Luisa sat in back, keeping a wary eye on her precious vinegar.

"It's a lovely sunny day for the fair," Mrs. Mallory commented as they drove off.

"*Si*," Luisa said happily. "It will be good for business."

Linda's eyes twinkled. Laughing, she said, "Even rain wouldn't stop people from buying your vinegar, Luisa." The housekeeper bobbed her head in delighted agreement.

Reaching the fair grounds, the trio were directed to their booth. At once Linda and her grandmother began decorating it. They twined Spanish fiesta-red, green, and yellow crepe paper streamers around the posts, and arranged festoons across the front. Then Linda fastened on big red paper roses of Seville, which Luisa had made. Next, Luisa set up her bottles on the counter.

By the time Mrs. Mallory and Linda had finished, it was almost ten o'clock. They stood back to appraise their handiwork.

Luisa was effusive in her admiration of the booth. "It is the most beautiful here!" she exclaimed.

"*Gracias.*" Mrs. Mallory smiled.

When the gates were opened, old customers flocked to purchase the allowed quota of two bottles of vinegar to a person. Many of them said, "We don't want to miss getting our share."

"Business is really brisk this year," Linda remarked gaily as she opened another box.

A little past noon activity dwindled, however, then ceased entirely.

"Everyone must be having lunch," Linda guessed.

Presently Mrs. Mallory went to eat with friends at a palm frond-sheltered refreshment patio. Linda purchased sandwiches, cake, and cold drinks there, and brought them back to the booth for her and Luisa. They ate quickly, expecting another rush of customers. But still no one came to make a purchase.

Luisa looked disturbed. "Why no one else buy?" she asked in a hurt voice, lovingly patting a bottle of chili vinegar. "I taste it, and taste it. It taste good like always. I think even maybe a little better."

"It's still the lull of the noon hour," Linda assured her. "Before the fair closes at midnight, you are going to wish that you had at least a hundred bottles more to sell."

Luisa sighed. "It has always been so."

At that moment a tall, thin man with a heavy mustache, bushy beard, and sideburns ambled toward the booth.

"Could be a customer," Luisa whispered uncertainly.

"Possibly," replied Linda. "I saw him talking to some people across the way, then they went off. Perhaps he runs some sort of concession and is drumming up customers."

The bearded man greeted them by inquiring affably, "Business good?"

"It has been," replied Linda. "Right now things are slow. I'm sure sales will pick up."

"Don't be too sure," the stranger warned.

"What you mean?" demanded Luisa, bristling.

The man shrugged and replied in a patient tone, "Lady, I only came to tell you there's a fellow with a booth down at the south edge of the grounds selling what he is claiming is the real chili vinegar, and telling everyone that your product is a cheap substitute."

Luisa burst out in a torrent of Spanish, then said, "He is a—a fake!"

"He certainly is, and should be stopped immediately!" exclaimed Linda indignantly. "I'll go find a fair grounds officer at once!"

"How about coming along with me first, and I'll show you where the other booth is," the stranger offered.

"I go. I hit that man over the head with his fake bottle," Luisa said vehemently and urged Linda to accompany them.

"Well, all right," Linda agreed. "But I must tell Dona first."

She hurried over to where Mrs. Mallory sat talking with her friends. Linda informed her in low tones of the competitive chili vinegar seller, and asked, "Would you please stay in the booth while Luisa and I go to investigate? I have a hunch he is a fraud."

"Indeed yes," replied Dona, concerned. "No wonder we suddenly lost customers."

A few minutes later Linda and Luisa, with their bearded informant, approached a small, enclosed, umbrella-type tent at the very edge of the grounds. It was a good distance from the main concessions.

"Here?" exclaimed Linda. "Why, this is no booth!"

"And where are all the customers who do not come to ours?" questioned Luisa, noticing there was no one around the tent.

"You'll see," said their guide. "Step right in."

"No, thank you," said Linda, her suspicions immediately aroused and her palms going clammy.

She stepped back to turn away when suddenly both she and Luisa were violently pushed from behind into the tent.

"What—!" Linda burst out, and stopped with a gasp. Confronting them, a leer on his face, stood Rod Coleman!

"Greetings," he said with an exaggerated bow.

"You!" Linda cried in shocked surprise.

Luisa's eyes were filled with fear and bafflement. "Who—who is this man?" she asked Linda.

"One of the masked men who broke into del Sol —and also held Bob and me prisoners!" Linda's eyes blazed.

Coleman gave a harsh laugh. "You won't give us the slip so easily this time, young lady," he said ominously.

Luisa forgot her own fear at this threat to Linda and started furiously toward Coleman.

"You wicked man!" she cried. "I teach you a lesson!"

Coleman snatched a club from under his jacket. "Stop!" he commanded roughly.

Linda reached out and pulled Luisa protectively beside her.

Rod Coleman glared at them. "Don't scream for help or I'll use this!"

From Linda's past experience she did not doubt but that he meant business. "What do you want, anyway!" she asked defiantly.

"You tell me where those Perez jewels are," Coleman demanded surlily.

"Why—why *you* have them," said Linda incredulously.

"There were no jewels in the chest, or the ranch house, and you know it," he growled. "The secret compartment was empty."

"If that is so," said Linda coolly, "then the old story must be true that my ancestor, Rosalinda Perez, sent the jewels back to Spain."

"Hogwash!" blurted Rod Coleman. "You know where those jewels are. You're next in line to inherit them. Talk now or we'll hold you both until you do."

"The whereabouts of the jewels is a complete mystery to me and everyone in my family," insisted Linda.

"She—she know nothing," Luisa added bravely.

"You shut up!" barked Coleman. Then he turned his head and asked out of the corner of his mouth, "All ready back there?"

The bearded man, who had remained silent at the rear of the tent, opened the back flap. An enclosed delivery truck was revealed. Linda's quick eyes also noted that one side of the man's beard was askew.

"He's wearing a disguise!" she thought. "His beard is false and probably his mustache, too! Who can he be?"

"Okay, you two!" snapped Coleman. "March!" He pointed to the truck.

Reluctantly Linda and Luisa walked toward the vehicle. Coleman and the other man grabbed hold of the captives and thrust them into the rear section of the truck.

"Stay put and don't make any noise," Coleman snarled, "if you know what's good for you!"

With that he slammed the panel doors shut. Linda and Luisa, clinging together, were engulfed by darkness. The next moment they were thrown to the floor as the truck started up with a lurch and drove off.

XI

The Sheriff's Clue

Luisa struggled to her knees, frantically pawing at the floor of the moving vehicle and screaming.

Linda caught hold of her and gave the Mexican woman a gentle shake. "Don't, Luisa, don't!" she urged kindly. "We're going to be all right. We'll escape somehow."

Luisa ceased her wailing and slumped again to the floor. "But how we escape?" she asked despairingly.

"We'll have to figure it out," replied Linda with more assurance than she felt. "Crying won't do it."

Luisa sat up straight, her usual determined spirit returning. "So right."

The two were silent for a while, each concentrating on possible means of escape. Finally Linda leaned over and whispered, "Luisa, you start pounding on the sides—keep it up while I investigate."

The Mexican woman scrambled to her feet, rocking precariously at the movement of the truck, and shouted, "I fix heem!"

She floundered to the cab and beat her fists against the wall. Repeatedly she cried out loudly in her native tongue.

Linda understood her, of course, and wondered if the driver knew what she was saying. The truck slowed to a stop, and Linda trembled, afraid that the man was coming back to tie them up. But the vehicle went on.

"It was probably a traffic stop," the girl thought.

Linda's mind began to spin. There would be other stops—a chance to escape if they could only open the door! She made her way over to Luisa and in a low tone said, "Keep pounding! Keep talking! Meanwhile I'll look for a way out."

Linda crept on hands and knees to the rear of the truck. Reaching up, she felt in the darkness for a lock mechanism on the doors. Her fingers touched a catch.

Cautiously Linda tried this, and the door opened a crack. "Oh, what wonderful luck!" she thought.

Linda scrambled back to Luisa and whispered her discovery. "We'll have to wait for the truck to slow down," she went on, "then jump out."

"*Bueno!*" exclaimed Luisa. "I will jump like my Geraldine and Genevieve!"

Despite herself, Linda giggled, then said seriously, "We'd better keep on talking, so the driver won't suspect anything. I'm sure he can hear what we're saying if we raise our voices."

The captives began to discuss, in loud tones, where they might be going. Linda said dramatically, "I'm afraid we'll never see the ranch again."

Luisa took the cue. "*O mio, mio!*" she groaned. "It is too terrible to think of!"

What seemed like hours elapsed before the truck slackened speed and stopped. "Now's our chance!" Linda hissed, pulling Luisa quickly to the rear.

The girl flicked the catch and the doors swung open, revealing a deserted road. At the same moment came the sound of an approaching train. They were at a railroad crossing.

"Lucky break for us," she thought as a long freight began to thunder past. "We have plenty of time."

"Jump!" Linda commanded.

Luisa obeyed, with agility surprising for one so plump. Linda followed, leaping onto the hard surface beside the Mexican woman. They fled toward a dense cluster of trees bordering the road. Linda peered out and managed to note the license number of the delivery truck, but could not get a clear glimpse of the driver. As soon as the freight had gone past, the truck started up and sped off down the road.

Suddenly the full relief at their escape hit Linda and Luisa. They hugged each other in delight. "All our talk did the trick!" Linda grinned. "That driver still thinks we're safely locked in. With the noise of the freight and his own engine, he didn't hear *us*."

Luisa laughed heartily. "Maybe he not hear so good anyhow."

"Now," said Linda, "we must find out exactly where we are and how to get back to the fair. Dona will be frantic."

Luisa looked down the strange road and said, "I not know where we are."

The two ventured out from the woods. The area seemed to be sparsely populated. There were occasional abandoned citrus orchards and wooded spots. In the distance could be seen rugged hills.

"No cars. No ride," Luisa grumbled.

"We'll have to keep walking until we can pick up one," said Linda.

Luisa sighed. "Is too much for fat lady."

"Maybe you'll lose a pound," Linda said consolingly. "I lose, yes," said Luisa. "But walking make me hungry, so I eat it back." She laughed good-naturedly.

They walked some distance without a single car passing them. Finally they arrived at a small farms section with a little more activity. There was a fruit and vegetable stand at a crossroads where two women had just driven up.

As they alighted, Linda said to Luisa, "I'll ask them if they'll take us back to the fair grounds."

"I pray they do." Luisa sighed again. "My feet hurt."

Linda hurried to the stand and approached the woman who had been driving. "Pardon me, I'm Linda Craig," she said with a friendly smile. "This is Luisa Alvarez. We were kidnaped from the Santa Clarita Guild Fair. Could you possibly return us there if you're heading that way?"

"Kidnaped!" exclaimed both women in amazement.

"How?" asked the driver dubiously.

"And why?" spoke up the other woman, obviously skeptical.

Linda briefly explained how they had been captured and forced into the delivery truck. At the end of her story both women, convinced it was true, were horrified and more than willing to help.

"Of course we'll drive you to the fair," said the owner of the car. "I've heard of a famous chili vinegar they sell there. I would like to buy some."

"Luisa makes it," Linda told them.

"You give us ride—I give you some bottles," Luisa assured the women happily.

Quickly the four climbed into the automobile. Luisa sank into the back seat with a great sigh of relief, slipped off her shoes, and wiggled her toes. "*O mio*, this is good!" she exclaimed.

Within the hour Linda and Luisa were back at the fair grounds. It was now late afternoon. The faces of

Dona and several friends who had come to stay with her turned suddenly from deep concern to gladness.

"Where have you been?" Mrs. Mallory asked Linda. "I've been very worried. I can tell by your face there has been trouble."

"A lot of trouble, I'm afraid," Linda replied. After introducing the women with her, she hastily told what had happened. Luisa interrupted now and then to say how brave "her young lady" had been.

Linda squeezed the housekeeper's arm. "*You* were wonderful—I'm sorry you had to go through such a frightening experience, but I'm thankful you were with me."

Dona expressed shock and dismay at the attempted kidnaping. "I should have realized there was something suspicious about that bearded man's story," she reproached herself.

"At least," Linda said, "I learned that Rod Coleman apparently did not locate the jewels. But he won't believe we don't know where they are."

"*Sí*, it is so," Luisa averred solemnly with a shiver. "I fear that *hombre* make big trouble—be very angry when he find out we get away."

Linda agreed. "We all will have to be constantly on our guard at the ranch and everywhere else. But what a lot I'll have to tell the sheriff!"

Mrs. Mallory explained that many people had come to the booth, reporting they had been warned by the stranger that Luisa's vinegar was spoiled. "I know now he did it to keep customers away so you and Luisa would leave to investigate."

Dona related that finally she had persuaded fair-goers that the man's story was false. "I guess word was passed around," she concluded. "As you can see, our counter is bare."

Luisa, although pleased, asked in a worried voice, "The vinegar—it is all sold? I promised some to these nice ladies for driving us."

Dona smiled. "Luckily there are a few bottles left in one of the boxes. I was so upset at your not returning, I neglected to put them out."

"I get." Luisa beamed. She brought out the remaining bottles and gave two each to the women who had brought them. "*Gracias* for ride," she said.

Linda and Mrs. Mallory also thanked the women warmly. As soon as they had gone off, Linda said she would phone the sheriff's office.

"Yes, you must do that," said Dona. "But please return as quickly as possible."

Linda smiled and nodded. "No long trips for me this time!"

She went to the fair grounds office and called the sheriff, giving him a full account of the kidnaping and her meeting with Rod Coleman. Linda described the false-bearded stranger and the delivery truck, reporting the license number.

"Fine work," he said. "I'm glad you got away."

The official assured Linda that he would dispatch

deputies to follow the road the delivery truck had taken. In addition, other men would be sent to the fair grounds immediately to pick up what clues they might find around the tent, and to lift imprints left by the truck's tires.

"I'll be in touch with you the minute we have any news," he promised. Linda thanked him and hung up. One of the fair ground officers, Mr. Donovan, who had listened with interest to the girl's report, asked her, "Just where is this tent? I don't remember seeing it."

"I'll show you," Linda offered.

She walked with the officer to the south edge of the grounds and stopped in surprise. "It's gone!" Linda exclaimed. "It was right there." She pointed to the spot.

"That figures," said Donovan. "It was apparently put up to decoy you, and taken down right afterward. I'll wait here until the sheriff's deputies arrive, and give them a hand."

Linda returned to the booth to find Mrs. Mallory and Luisa taking down the decorations. At once Linda began to help.

Dona gave her a smile. "I assume you are ready to go home, dear," she said, "or do you wish to spend the evening at the fair?"

"No, thank you." Linda half sighed, half laughed. "I've had enough activity for today."

"I've had enough for *all* days." Luisa groaned, pulling down streamers.

"I am happy," said Mrs. Mallory, "that our booth made better than its usual amount of money for the Guild."

"Is good." Luisa's face brightened with its usual broad smile.

"Chili vinegar very good," Linda said, her eyes twinkling. "Let's go home!"

Later that evening a phone call came to del Sol from the sheriff. Linda took it.

"We've learned," he told her, "that the license of the delivery truck was issued to a Peter J. Henry of San Francisco."

Linda mulled over the name until a theory occurred to her. "Could Hank Trask, the Colemans' accomplice, be an alias of Peter J. Henry?" she asked. "Hank is a nickname for Henry."

"A good probability," the officer conceded. "I'll work on that angle."

He went on to tell Linda that no trace had been found of the bushy-bearded stranger, the truck, or its driver. "I figure that as soon as they discovered your escape, they immediately hid out in some obscure spot."

The sheriff asked Linda if she thought Trask was the driver. "I really can't say," she replied. "I never did get a good look at the man behind the wheel."

The next morning Linda and Bob went to the

Highway House to pay Kathy a visit. She was resting in a deck chair on the back patio. To her friends' relief Kathy seemed a great deal better, both in appearance and spirits. Her eyes were dancing brightly, and her face had its natural warm apricot hue.

"I can't keep her in bed," lamented Mrs. Hamilton, smiling nevertheless.

Kathy grinned. "I'm rarin' to ride—any minute now!"

"Tie her down," Bob advised, and chuckled. "If she won't lie flat for the next couple of days, that is."

"Fine pal you are!" pouted Kathy playfully.

When Linda told her about the previous day's kidnaping, Kathy's face clouded over with fear. "To think of you in such danger and me here not being a shred of help!"

Mrs. Hamilton shuddered. "The whole situation is so sinister. Those awful men seem to know every move you Craigs make."

Bob's jaw tightened. "They're a foxy bunch all right, but foxes usually get trapped sooner or later."

Talk presently turned to the Trail Blazers Club 28. "Now that our papers and pictures are safely in Los Angeles," Bob said, "we should receive our certificates soon."

Half an hour later the Craigs left. That afternoon Linda worked Chica in the ring, putting her through only the exercises which she would be called upon to execute at the big show: the walk, trot, canter, reverse, figure eight, pivot, and back.

Bob had perched on the top rail of the fence to watch. "That horse is perfect, just perfect," he declared.

"Yes," Linda admitted. "But Chica d'Oro has to be better than perfect so that no matter what strange sound or sight may occur, she won't hesitate an instant in her responses to commands."

"My money is on Chica." Bob grinned. "And the hand that is guiding her."

Linda flashed him an appreciative smile, then tilted her chin and told him saucily, "Flattery will get you nowhere, buddy boy."

"Oh no?" he retorted.

On Tuesday Linda and Bob received their handsome parchment Certificates of Membership in the Trail Blazers organization. Kathy and Larry phoned to say that they too had theirs.

Linda laughed gaily. "A hard-won victory," she remarked to Bob. "But worth each struggle."

"You bet," her brother agreed.

A little later Linda stood before the portrait of Rosalinda Perez as she often did when especially happy, and spoke softly in Spanish to her likeness:

"I hope, dear Great-Great-Grandmother, that I may continue to live up to our name as you would wish me to do. And how glad I am that those wicked thieves did not find your beautiful jewels. You hid them well."

As often happened, Linda thought the beautiful woman smiled at her as if wanting to help.

That evening after dinner Sue Mason phoned to tell Linda, "Be ready, all you new Trail Blazers, to start out Saturday morning on our first tracking ride. We're going after those rustlers for keeps this time. They're still hiding out and stealing cattle!"

XII

Rustler Hunt

During the next three days Linda divided much of her time between working Chica d'Oro and talking on the phone. The Trail Blazers Club 28 members kept busy discussing plans for the rustler-tracking ride on Saturday. Linda relayed the various conversations to her brother, who was helping to reroof the barn. The most important was that of Chuck Eller.

"He says," reported Linda, "that two men were seen the other night right after a calf snatching. It was at a small ranch not far from the entrance to our Crespi Cove trail. But the men ran away, and it was too dark for anyone to see what they looked like."

"Those could be the two who raided Carl Johnson's cabin," said Bob. "They must still be working in that vicinity. The dense woods provide perfect hideouts."

"Perhaps we ought to pay Carl a visit first thing on our ride to find out if he has seen those men again," suggested Linda. "We might be able to pick up some good clues."

"I'll go along with that," said Bob. "Why not talk it over with Chuck? Also, ask him if he doesn't think the bunch should start out from del Sol. We're the most centrally located."

Linda hurried off to do this and Chuck concurred enthusiastically with her suggestions. Early Saturday morning Bob drove over to the Highway House with an empty horse trailer to get Kathy and Patches.

"Are you sure you feel up to this trip?" he asked her. "It may be rugged."

"Positive! I'm feeling great, really, and rarin' to ride." Kathy grinned. "Rustlers, here I come!"

As Bob and Kathy drove into Rancho del Sol, a big stock truck owned by the father of a member pulled in with ten horses loaded sidewise, head to tail. Their riders followed in two cars, with Larry directly behind them. Chuck came next with Sue Mason and their horses. Finally, eighteen young people had gathered, chattering and laughing noisily about the trip.

"Are you sheriff's deputies ready?" the president called out with a grin.

Larry slapped one hand on an imaginary holster, whipped out an invisible gun, and pointed it toward the distant hills. "I'm a dead shot!" he announced.

Another boy, Bill Winters, bent low and made a pretense of scrutinizing the ground with a magnifying glass. "I sure don't see suspicious boot prints," he announced. "But give me time, give me time!"

Amid the general laughter Chuck called out, "Tallyho!"

The Trail Blazers scrambled for their cars. Linda and Bob ran back to bid good-by to Dona and Bronco who had come out to watch the proceedings and wish the riders luck.

"Please be careful," Dona admonished them.

Bronco added, "Keep a sharp eye out at all times."

"We'll do both," Linda promised. Rango stood beside the Mallorys wagging his tail wistfully and barking reproachfully at being left behind. "You're needed here, old boy, to act as guard and keep away intruders," Linda told him.

Cactus Mac hurried from the corral waving his big, well-worn stetson. "Bring back those *diablos*," he called to the Craigs and their friends.

The caravan moved out with Bob and Linda leading, since they knew the route. After a while the cars pulled into the wide parking area behind the service station's garage on the valley speedway. Bob introduced Chuck to the young mechanic who had fixed the trailer wheel, and the attendant agreed to keep an eye on the riders' vehicles during their absence.

Finally the Club 28 members saddled up and started along the trail which Linda's foursome had blazed. Chuck, directly behind the Craigs, said, "I certainly recognize this route from your excellent map and pictures."

As the procession drew near Carl Johnson's cabin, his two big dogs barked excited notice of the callers' approach.

"I'm glad those animals decided to come home," said Kathy.

As before, Carl Johnson ran out of the cabin gripping his rifle. Then, seeing Linda and the others, his face broke into a happy smile and he put the gun aside. Bob introduced the elderly man to the riders, who sang out a chorus of greetings.

"Why didn't you send me a wire sayin' you Trail Blazers was ridin' this way?" Carl asked with a wry grin. "I would've hooked a whole pailful o' trout!"

"Thanks anyway," said Linda, smiling warmly. "We'll take a rain check."

"What we're really here to find out, Mr. Johnson," Bob explained, "is whether or not you've discovered anything more about those men who robbed your larder. Have you seen them again?"

Quick anger colored Carl's face. "They came back," he blurted. "I seen 'em, and I sure 'nough found out somethin'." He grinned cagily. "But them two didn't see me. I'd just come back from gettin' me a brace o' rabbits over the hill, and I seen smoke comin' out o' my stovepipe."

He winked. "I wasn't takin' any chances walkin' into the varmints, so I sneaked up Injun-style to the

146

open window in back, and peeped in. And there was those same two grub-liners settin' down to my table scroungin' my bacon 'n' eggs."

"Then what happened?" Linda asked excitedly.

"The two galoots was hatchin' some skulduggery," Carl continued. "I heard the one call that ugly, flat-nosed coyote Max, and Max called t'other Sam. They was talkin' pretty cocky about their beef hauls—said they'd hit X next. Finished eatin' and left right off without so much as cleanin' up."

"At least," Linda remarked, "we know the men's first names, and no doubt they're the rustlers."

"True," said Bob. "Wonder what they meant by hitting X."

Larry spoke up. "I think I know. There's a ranch named the Three X just over the hill a little off the highway. I've noticed the R.F.D. mailbox there when I've driven by. The name on it is Turnbull."

"You could be right," said Chuck. "That's in the vicinity of the last rustling activity."

"What's our next move, leader?" asked Kathy.

"We'll break up into three small groups," Chuck directed. "Each will ride in from different directions toward the outskirts of Three X, searching the woods and canyons, then converge on the ranch buildings together."

The Craigs thanked Carl Johnson for his information. "Anytime I can help pin down those varmints," he said, "let me know."

The Trail Blazers quickly formed their groups, with Chuck Ellers and Sue Mason joining the Craigs, Kathy, and Larry. They all rode back to the highway and crossed it into the property of the Three X ranch. Here the three sections went their separate ways.

Linda and her fellow riders carefully looked for footprints along their designated route, and searched behind clumps of dense brush, but saw no trace of any trespassers. As Linda and her friends drew near the ranch proper, they noticed a herd of whiteface cattle peacefully grazing in a field.

When they came in sight of the buildings, Linda said in surprise, "The place seems deserted!"

"Let's ride in as slowly and noiselessly as possible behind the big barn," Chuck suggested. "We'll be pretty well obscured from view and can get a better look around."

They reined to a stop near one side of the barn and scanned the area. Then the riders exchanged startled glances upon hearing men's loud, argumentative voices inside the structure.

One was exclaiming, "You're loco, plumb loco to try runnin' off a bunch in broad daylight. I tell you we got to wait 'til dark."

A second voice shouted, "No such thing! Everyone's gone from here. You saw 'em all leave in the car except Mr. Turnbull and he's way off mending fence. We can cut out half a dozen fat head from the herd, and have 'em up in that brush corral of ours long before those ranch folks get back. Come on!"

The next moment the listeners heard the sound of heavy stomping toward the front of the barn.

Chuck quickly dismounted. "Let's intercept them," he urged Bob and Larry. "You girls hold the horses."

The boys hastened around in time to confront two men emerging from the wide doorway. One, short and stocky with a broad nose, was grumbling to his taller companion.

"Stop where you are, Max and Sam!" Bob commanded.

The stocky man fell back a step, astounded. "You know us?"

"We do," said Chuck, and called loudly, "*Tallyho! Tallyho!*"

The suspects turned to flee, but before they could the three girls rode up swiftly, blocking the men's path. The boys seized the pair, and Linda tossed a coil of rope from Bob's saddle horn to them. Just as the captives were securely bound, the other Trail Blazers came at full gallop from all directions, encircling the area. With one group was the rancher who had been out mending fence and had been told by them of the club's suspicions.

"Here are the rustlers—in person," Chuck told Mr. Turnbull as he arrived. "Max and Sam. They were all set to run off a half dozen head of your cattle. We overheard their plan."

"I told you we should've waited 'til dark," whined Sam to his pal.

"Shut up!" growled Max.

"Well, I sure can't thank you young people enough," exclaimed the grateful rancher. "I'll call the sheriff pronto!" He hurried into the house.

The Craigs and their companions were highly praised for capturing the men. Within half an hour a siren announced the coming of a police car. It pulled up and two deputies leaped out. Immediately they snapped handcuffs on the prisoners before untying them.

The men sullenly gave their full names as Max Velt and Sam Rout, and confessed to the rustling charges against them. Their shaggy brown horses were tethered in a thicket, and the officers instructed the rancher to impound them until further notice. Then the deputies sped away with their captives.

Chuck Ellers turned to the Trail Blazers. "Well, old-timers, what about a rousing cheer for our new members whose clues led us to make the capture of these rustlers?"

Hats went into the air, and a loud chorus of "Hip-hip hoorays!" rang out.

Mr. Turnbull raised his stetson high and shouted, "Hooray for all of you!"

It was now past noon and Chuck asked him, "Mind if we picnic somewhere on your property?"

"I'd be honored," replied the ranch owner. "Down

yonder in that clump of cottonwoods is a big water hole. Crystal-clear water too. It's a right nice place for a picnic."

They thanked him and rode to the pretty, shaded spot. The Trail Blazers had brought halters and tie ropes on their saddles. Now they unbridled the horses and secured them to trees. The long lines enabled the animals to amble about, graze, and drink. Finally the riders unsaddled their mounts and settled down on the grassy floor to eat the lunches they had brought.

"I'm absolutely ravenous!" Linda exclaimed.

Larry eyed his sandwich appreciatively. "Me too. Rustler hunting sure makes a fellow hollow inside!"

As the Trail Blazers finished eating, the rancher appeared with several huge watermelons. He cut slices of the ice-cold fruit and passed them around.

When Mr. Turnbull came to the Craigs, he remarked, "You know, I caught another pair of fellows one morning that I figured might be those rustlers. They'd been sleeping in the barn. But apparently shelter for the night was all they wanted, so I didn't call the sheriff. The men took off in a hurry, though."

"What do they look like?" Linda asked quickly.

Mr. Turnbull gave a good description: One man was stocky and had brown hair; his companion was tall, gaunt, and bony-faced.

"Rod Coleman and Hank Trask!" Linda gasped.

151

"You've met up with those two?" the rancher asked in surprise.

"Yes," Bob replied, frowning. "They match the description of a couple of prowlers who broke into our ranch house."

"Well, now, I guess I *should* have had 'em picked up," said Mr. Turnbull soberly. "But I had no special reason to suspect the men. I run saddle tramps off my place every once in a while." He narrowed his eyes thoughtfully. "Come to think of it, that pair didn't look like wandering cowboys. And they did some pretty fancy talking."

"Do you remember what they said?" asked Linda.

"Partly," the rancher replied. "The bony-faced fellow called Hank Trask bragged he was a direct descendant of a servant on Rancho del Sol when the first Spanish family, the Perezes, lived there. Claimed he had some valuable family jewels due him."

"What!" Linda cried in astonishment and dismay.

Bob too was taken aback by this revelation. He explained to their host, "We live at del Sol. My sister and I are descendants of the Perezes."

"Well, I'll be rope-tied!" Mr. Turnbull exclaimed, beaming. "I'm mighty glad I had a chance to meet you folks and alert you to those fellows."

"So are we," Bob declared. "Coleman and Trask will stop at nothing."

"I'll keep my eyes open in case they show up again," the friendly rancher promised. "Well, got to get to work. You young people keep on enjoying yourselves. And ride back any time you've a mind to."

"Thank you very much," said Linda.

As soon as he had left, she went on, "Bob, that old note left in Chica's stall the day she was injured must be authentic! To think that awful Hank Trask has a claim to some of our family's jewels!"

Bob looked perplexed. "But why doesn't Trask just come forward and demand his rightful share?" he asked.

"Because," Linda conjectured, "he's in league with the Colemans, who have persuaded him to get hold of the whole collection."

"At least they haven't found the jewels yet," Bob reminded her. "And I don't think they ever will, if Rosalinda Perez sent the treasure back to Spain."

Their discussion was interrupted by Chuck Ellers, who motioned the Craigs forward. The rest of the Club 28 members had formed a semicircle around their president. Silence prevailed as Linda and Bob stood facing them wonderingly.

Chuck began speaking with a broad grin. "Since all of our board members are present," he said, "and a representative number of regular members, we've just held a special meeting. There was a unanimous vote to ask Linda Craig, as a delegate of Club 28, to compete in the annual contest at the big Trail Blazers show for selection of their queen."

The members clapped and cheered loudly.

"Oh!" Linda gasped. "I—I'm deeply honored—and overwhelmed. I'm not sure I can qualify." She had assumed that Sue Mason would be chosen to represent their club.

Sue spoke up promptly. "None of us has a speck of doubt. You are the best horsewoman in our group. And Chica d'Oro is the most qualified horse."

Linda blushed with embarrassed pleasure. "Well, thanks a million. Chica and I will do our very best," she said fervently.

Shortly afterward, tired, but happy at their successful mission, the riders saddled up and rode to their outfits at the gas station.

Before Kathy left for home with Bob, she murmured to Linda, "Sue Mason has a list of most of the queen contestants chosen so far. Shirley Blaine has been selected by the Malibu Club."

"That figures," said Bob wryly. "She'll be tough competition, sis."

Linda raised her chin. "I'll be ready for her." Inwardly she was not so certain. Shirley, although frivolous and snobbish, had a reputation for being a skilled equestrienne.

A sudden thought struck Linda. "My goodness! The show is next week! I'll have to work Chica every minute I can."

Back at del Sol, the Craigs found the household calm and undisturbed by any new incidents. Bronco,

Dona, and Luisa were joyous over the capture of the rustlers and the news about Linda.

"I'm not surprised, though," said Bronco, glancing proudly at his granddaughter.

The Mallorys' enthusiasm was tempered somewhat when they learned of Hank Trask's claim to the Perez gems. Bronco frowned. "In that case, he and his Coleman cronies won't give up their search easily."

Despite this worry Linda went to bed exhilarated over the honor of being the representative of Club 28 in the queen contest. She was too excited to sleep soundly and at two in the morning was awakened by Rango barking. She sat up.

"What's going on at this hour?" Linda asked herself.

She jumped out of bed, ran to the window, and peered into pitch darkness. Not even the beam of a guard's flashlight could be seen.

"He must be making his rounds near the fence," Linda thought.

Rango's barking continued. It came from the front of the house. Quickly Linda put on her slippers and robe and ran into the hall. No one else was up. She hurried down the stairs. On the landing Linda froze.

Someone was tampering with the lock on the front door!

XIII

A Spiteful Hoax

For a few seconds Linda was frightened motionless. She heard the low voice of a man muttering about the dog's yapping.

Rango kept up his barking, which was coming closer. Frantically Linda wondered if the guard had been overpowered by this apparent housebreaker. Her heart thumping, she turned to race upstairs and awaken Bob and Bronco. At that moment she saw them coming down. Bronco signaled for her not to move and took a stand beside the light switch in the hall.

Suddenly the door was unlocked and pushed open. A tall figure entered stealthily and closed the door quickly. Rango, left just outside, gave sharp protesting yelps. Bronco snapped on the lights.

"Hank Trask!" gasped Linda.

The intruder turned to bolt outside, but Bob dashed forward and grabbed him. He struggled viciously to break free, but Bronco's strong hands also seized him. Realizing he was outnumbered, Trask ceased to resist.

Just then the door burst open and one of the guards, named Scott, entered on the run, with Rango leaping ahead of him.

"This fellow break in?" Scott asked, out of breath.

"He did," replied Bronco tersely. "Where were you?"

"Out behind the hay shed, where I found a strange delivery truck," the guard replied. "I was hunting for the driver around there when I heard Rango barking and came to investigate." He shook out handcuffs and snapped them on Trask's wrists.

Hank Trask glowered. "You've got no right to do this," he snarled. "I came here to get my inherited jewels you've all cheated me out of!"

At this moment Dona Mallory appeared at the head of the stairs. Although startled at the scene before her, the stately woman said in icy tones:

"You may have a claim to the Perez jewels, but unfortunately for you and my family, their whereabouts are a complete mystery."

Trask scoffed, "You expect me to believe that?" He straightened his bony frame with a swagger, and stared about arrogantly with his piercing light blue eyes. "You better be handing me over my share or else give me its worth in money. If not, I'll hire me a good lawyer to get my due."

"Your only due is a long jail sentence for kidnaping and housebreaking," Bronco curtly told him. "And the only kind of lawyer you'll be needing is a defense lawyer."

Linda, hoping to catch the captive off guard, said abruptly, "Your delivery truck is registered in your own name, Peter J. Henry, of San Francisco! Why the alias?"

A flicker of fear showed in Trask's eyes but he remained stubbornly silent.

Bob asked him, "Where are your friends the Colemans hiding out? If you do a little talking, things may go easier with you."

"I got nothing to say about nobody to nobody," muttered Trask, and pressed his thin lips tightly.

Rango had been standing in front of Trask uttering low throaty growls. "It's all right now, Rango," said Linda, patting him. "You were a mighty good watchdog to keep trailing this trespasser and barking to waken us."

"Let's go!" Scott snapped to Trask and firmly ushered him outside.

Bronco hurried to telephone Deputy Sheriff Randall and report the capture. "We'll take good care of Trask—behind bars," Randall said emphatically. "I'll concentrate on rounding up the Coleman brothers."

That morning the family went to church in Lockwood, then relaxed for a while on the patio.

Dona said, puzzled, "I cannot understand what

possessed Mr. Trask to come here again, since he had searched our house with his partners before. It was such a reckless thing to do."

"Perhaps," said Bob, "he figured he was losing out too much by tying in with the Colemans, and wanted to have a look around here on his own."

Linda shuddered. "It seems horrible to think that any of Great-Great-Grandmother's beautiful jewels might ever be going to that dishonest man."

"Well, don't lose any sleep over it," said Bob. "The jewels evidently aren't going to anyone."

Later, Linda spent some time with Chica, brushing the palomino and talking to her.

"And now for a short workout," she said. "No tricks this week, baby. All you're going to be asked is to give a perfect performance."

She reached down and patted Chica on the shoulder. At once the filly pulled back her foot with a bent knee and went into a low bow.

"You ham!" Linda laughed, then added soberly, "But I'm glad you gave me this warning. You're such a smart horse I'll have to watch my hand during the big show so as not to give you any signals. Highly schooled stunts would go against you instead of building up points for us."

During the next two hours Linda made the filly walk, trot, canter, and gallop. At the end she hugged her. "Very good, but tomorrow you must hold your head more erect."

The following morning Linda checked the costumes she and Bob would wear in the contest. Bob was to be dressed in frontier pants of a mocha shade, brown boots, a white western shirt with a tan tie, and a white hat.

Linda's suit was kelly green with bell bottom pants embroidered up the sides and jeweled, as was the yoke of her fringed white leather shirt. Green was the most striking color she could wear on her golden palomino. Linda would wear white boots, gloves, tie, and hat with a jeweled border and hatband. She was satisfied that everything was spotless.

"I think we'll look well," Linda concluded. "If only our performance measures up to our clothes!"

While she was giving Chica a lesson in holding up her head when standing still but not being reined up tautly, Bob was exercising Rocket in the ring. The ranch horse seemed to regard the whole procedure as a lot of nonsense—he was not going anywhere and he was not working any cattle!

"Rocket doesn't approve of this business," Bob said to his sister with a laugh. "I have a feeling we won't be very proud of ourselves."

"Well, at least you'll help fill up a couple of classes," Linda comforted him. "You know there have to be so many in a class in order to hold it."

"Anything to be obliging," Bob said. "That's us, Rocket, eh?" Rocket expressed his "obligingness" by bolting for the ring entrance.

160

On Thursday morning Linda received a call from the deputy sheriff's office. "Will you and your brother come to Lockwood and see if you can identify two men who have been arrested?" Randall asked.

"Yes indeed."

Excited, Linda called Bob from the corral and they drove to town. At Randall's office, in the small waiting room, the prisoners were brought before the Craigs.

"That's Rod Coleman!" Linda immediately pointed to the familiar figure of her former captor. "He and Hank Trask tied us up in the cabin."

Bob said, "I'm sure the other man is his brother Ben, from descriptions I've heard of him."

A clerk was taking notes at the desk. "Rod Coleman," he said aloud as he wrote. "Ben Coleman."

"*I* didn't say that was me," the huskier prisoner snarled.

Randall directed the clerk, "Leave it Ben Coleman."

Linda looked straight at Rod. "How do you explain your part in having me and our housekeeper kidnaped?"

"That wasn't my idea," Coleman insisted. "I was just doing a job for someone else for a fee."

"For Hank Trask?" prodded Linda. "That delivery truck belongs to him. He was the driver."

The Colemans glared at her. "You don't know that," growled Ben.

"We do know it," said Bob. "The police in San Francisco sent down the registration information—including Trask's real name."

The brothers were obviously startled. Linda next questioned the prisoners about the bushy-bearded stranger who had led her and Luisa to the tent and helped shove them into the delivery truck.

"Don't know," was Rod Coleman's sullen answer. "He's a friend of Trask's. All I ever heard is that the fellow don't have to worry about money."

"And paid you to do the job!" Linda exclaimed in disgust. "What was his motive in kidnaping us?"

The Colemans denied knowing the reason. Linda, however, overheard Ben mutter to his brother, "You were a fool to give your name to these kids in the first place."

"How was I to know they'd escape before we had a chance to find the jewels?" Rod retorted. "Anyway, we were going to change our names."

Nothing further could be learned from the men, so a waiting officer led them back to their cells.

"I think we've found out one thing," said Linda. "That bearded stranger must be the same man who paid Rod Coleman to injure Chica d'Oro, and also, he could be the mysterious diver at Crespi Cove. He has the same build."

"I'll go along with you on that theory," said Bob. "Now our only problem is to find out *who* he is, and why he did those things."

162

Early Friday afternoon Bob, Linda, Larry, and Kathy were ready to roll out of Rancho del Sol and head for Cowboy Park and the Trail Blazers All Clubs Show. To the two cars were attached the horse trailers. At the park the girls would use the dressing room in front of Chica's quarters, and the boys would sleep in the other trailer.

By the time the del Sol caravan arrived at the park, outfits were coming in from all directions. The spacious area, alive with an excited hustle, was perfect for such a large gathering of people and horses.

There was a fine arena with a covered grandstand and bleachers. To one side was a grassy, dust-free, ten-acre parking lot for club contestants. In the rear of the grandstand a catering service had set up long tables, and near them a portable floor had been laid for dancing.

The foursome was greeted by Chuck Ellers at the check-in gate. "Follow me," he told them, and led the way to a pleasant oak-shaded spot at the rear of the lot.

Sue Mason was there waiting. "I've been doing sentinel duty," she announced gaily. "I really had to guard this place to hold it for you."

"Oh thank you. It's perfect," said Linda.

Many of the people coming in for the show brought house trailers. Other participants, arriving with their families, set up tents. The horses were tied to the backs of the trailers and blanketed with day sheets to keep them clean. The Craigs and their friends went around introducing themselves to others, while the horses, affected by the air of excitement, kept whinnying back and forth.

"This is more fun than I ever could have imagined!" exclaimed Linda, stars sparkling in her dark eyes.

She and her companions remained for the alfresco supper and dancing, which most of the other Club 28 members attended. All of the queen representatives were there except Shirley Blaine. Linda found the girls to be full of fun and good sportsmanship.

"Where is Shirley?" she asked.

"I understand she's staying at a de luxe unit in the Silver Saddle Motel," one of the girls spoke up. "She's boarding her horse and groom at the fancy Sierra Stables!"

Jill Raymond, a petite girl, who was the queen contestant from the Bell Gardens Club, sighed and said, "Shirley's sure to be chosen queen. With her striking looks, elegant clothes, fine trainer, trained horse, and top riding ability, how can she lose?"

Linda made no comment. Just being part of the big show and having been chosen as representative of Club 28 meant a lot to her. Of course she and Chica d'Oro would try to bring honor to their group by winning if possible.

The dancing concluded at ten o'clock so that participants for the following day's horse show could get their needed rest. The runoff of the various classes would start at nine in the morning.

The queens were not to participate in any of the regular events. For this reason Linda dressed in jeans and plaid shirt, then helped Kathy get ready. How attractive the blond girl looked wearing a plain burnt orange western suit with brown boots, tie, and hat, and riding on brown and white Patches!

Larry wore tan frontier pants, a yellow plaid western shirt, and brown boots, tie, and hat. He made a fine appearance on chestnut Jubilee, as did Bob in his mocha outfit on bay Rocket.

The trio filed into the arena for the first class, the Trail Class. Unfortunately none of them performed well in overcoming the obstacles. Patches kept backing off from the gate as Kathy reached to open it. Finally the judge ordered her to ride around it. The pinto flatly refused to walk over the calfskin, and broke her ground hitch when Kathy dismounted to open the mailbox.

Jubilee accepted all the challenges, but was cautious and slow. Rocket, being a natural trail horse, took the hazards with alacrity. But when it came to the walk, trot, and canter with the group around the breaking ring, true to form he showed his disgust by frequently breaking his gait.

Only one participant of the eleven entries was without fault—a young boy with a Morgan, and he won the trophy. Bob took a third place ribbon, Larry a fifth, and Kathy did not place.

In the Western Pleasure Class, Patches worked nicely around the ring, and Kathy took second prize. Larry won fourth, Bob did not place. He was the only one of the three, however, to enter the Ring-Spearing Class, and won the trophy.

Now and then Linda would run back to the lot and check on Chica d'Oro to make sure she was not being bothered. As her proud owner walked again toward the arena to watch the last event before lunch, she came face to face with Shirley Blaine. Linda greeted the girl pleasantly and would have gone on, but Shirley stopped her.

With a cheerful smile, she said, "Why, hello there, Linda Craig. I've been looking for you. I thought we might have a little chat before we start competing against each other in the ring."

"It won't be long now." Linda smiled, inwardly surprised at the other's sudden chumminess.

Shirley shrugged and said blithely, "May the best queen win!" Then she asked, "Will you be my guest for a spin down the highway for a soda? There's a little place near the junction."

"Why, thank you, but do you think we ought to leave now?" Linda demurred.

She did not want to go with the girl. Then she reproached herself—perhaps they had misjudged Shirley. After all, Shirley might be trying to make up for her snobbishness at their first encounter.

"Oh, come on!" Shirley urged. "A couple of the other queens are going to be there. We'll relax for a bit, and come back together."

"Well-l, all right," Linda acceded finally. "But we'll have to hurry."

"I'll step on it." Shirley laughed.

She was as good as her promise, Linda found out. Shirley kept her cream convertible at top speed. As they passed the Silver Saddle Motel coffee shop, Linda proposed, "Why not stop here? It's closer."

Shirley shook her head. "This other place is better," she stated and sped on.

During the drive Shirley had little to say. Linda made several attempts at conversation, but received only brief replies.

"She's certainly changeable," the ranch girl observed wryly to herself.

Finally Shirley stopped at a small roadside luncheonette about three miles from the park. "Here we are!" she announced. The girls alighted and went inside the small restaurant.

"No one else is here," remarked Linda as they seated themselves.

"They'll be along." Shirley laughed. "I guess I drove pretty fast." The next moment she jumped up saying, "I just remembered. I want to show you some pictures! They're honeys. Order chocolate malts, will you, while I get the pics from the car?"

She hurried out to the convertible. To Linda's utter amazement Shirley hopped in behind the wheel, turned the car around, and drove off.

Linda jumped up in shocked dismay. Now she knew the reason for Shirley's affability—a means to put Linda out of the competition!

The proprietress came over. "Is something wrong, young lady?" she asked, puzzled.

"Very much!" replied Linda. "I'm stranded! Is there anyone here who would drive me to Cowboy Park?"

"Not a soul," the woman replied. "My husband always goes out with the car at this time to load up at the produce market."

Linda's mind raced. Maybe if she could reach Cactus Mac he might get her to the contest in time. "May I use your phone?" she asked. Apologetically the woman replied that there was no telephone.

Linda was heartsick. In a panic she raced out to the road and looked up and down. Not a car in sight! Frantic, she started to run.

XIV

Queens Contest

In Cowboy Park, Bob, Kathy, and Larry had become frantic at Linda's prolonged absence. They had searched the area thoroughly and made inquiries of many people. None had seen Linda recently.

Finally Jill Raymond, who had been away from the park for half an hour, told them, "I think I saw Linda Craig go off a little while ago with Shirley Blaine in her car."

Bob and the others were mystified. "It's hard to believe," said Kathy, "that Shirley would take a chance missing the contest."

"She isn't around either," Bob noted.

"Oh-h!" cried Kathy, worriedly. "Do you suppose the girls have been in an accident?"

"I think one of us had better hurry down to that Silver Saddle Motel," said Bob. "Maybe Shirley and Linda are there."

"You go, Bob," said Larry. "I'll get Chica d'Oro

ready in case Linda shows up. There isn't much time left before the contest starts."

Already the other queen contestants, attractively costumed, were taking their places in the arena. Bob was about to leave when Kathy exclaimed, "Here comes Shirley!"

They all stared. Shirley, resplendent in a yellow jeweled tailored suit with gold accouterments— boots, gloves, tie, and hat—was mounted on a sorrel Arabian that showed savvy and training.

Kathy ran up to her and demanded, "Where is Linda?"

Shirley raised her eyebrows and replied in a surprised tone, "You don't mean to say she isn't here!" The Malibu girl rode away before Kathy could question her further.

A group of other contestants nearby chattered admiringly. Kathy heard one say, "Isn't Shirley gorgeous? Positively dazzling! She can't lose!"

Another remarked, "She'll be our next queen—no question about it!"

Angrily Kathy ran back to the trailers, where Bob and Larry were having a hard time with Chica. The palomino was nervous and unco-operative at Linda's absence, dancing about and refusing the bit.

The call came over the loud-speaker: "Queen competitors, get ready to ride!"

Kathy was almost in tears. "Oh, Linda, where are you?"

Finally the boys were able to lead Chica d'Oro to the rear of the arena just as another announcement blared out: "Contestants ride in!"

The colorful procession of forty beautiful young women astride their fine horses started to move. At that moment a farmer's truck roared into the park road, and an excited girl in shirt and jeans jumped out.

"Linda!" shouted Bob and the others joyously. Chica gave an excited, loud whinny of greeting.

Her young owner swung into the saddle, cheeks aflame with anger. "Thanks," she gasped. There was no time to say anything more.

Bob whipped out his handkerchief and wiped the dust off one of her boots. Larry did the same for the other as she took her place in the moving line.

"Good luck!" he whispered, and hurried with Bob and Kathy for seats in the grandstand.

Inside, the queens had started around the ring. When Shirley saw Linda, she gave a perceptible start and the brilliant smile she had been affecting vanished in a look of fear. Then she tossed her head haughtily and flicked some imaginary dirt from her suit as if to remind Linda that she could not win anyhow wearing her jeans.

Linda eyed her rival steadily, and made the silent vow: "I'm going to outride you, Shirley Blaine! Even if I lose on account of my clothes, I'm going to outride you."

They were going around the ring at a walk. Shirley, in her surprise upon seeing Linda, had involuntarily tightened suddenly on the reins. Her horse had made a quick little sideways step. Linda wondered if the judges had seen it.

The commands came for the trot and canter, the reverse, and walk, trot, and canter. As the queen contestants passed the grandstand, families and friends applauded for their favorite girl. But there came a general hearty hand clapping from all over the grandstand when Linda went by, as if the spectators were aware that some dire occurrence had prevented her from appearing in proper attire.

Although this warmed Linda's heart, she knew that it would have no influence on the tally of the judges. Performance, conformation of horse, and costume points were all that would be considered. So far, Chica d'Oro's performance had been perfect.

Linda did not look up into the stand, since this was not supposed to be done. But she could guess that the faces of the del Sol group wore puzzled expressions.

The contestants lined up at the far side of the arena, and the individual performances commenced. The girls rode in the order in which they had entered and were required to figure eight, pivot, and back.

Shirley was fourth. It was evident now that she was unusually tense. She held too tight a rein, which brought her horse to a standstill in the middle of its backing.

Linda and Chica d'Oro, in contrast, gave a flawless performance. The beautiful, well-trained palomino worked free, forward and straight, and passed smoothly from one step to another at the very instant of Linda's command.

The applause was thunderous. It meant one all-important thing to Linda—that she *had* outridden Shirley. But she knew her rival's points on costume would probably put the Malibu contestant ahead even with her one obvious fault, and even the possible two.

Most of the contenders had a couple or more faults against them. Three others, besides Linda, who had performed without a demerit had not, however, given smooth performances.

Linda fought back tears. "I haven't a chance against Shirley," she thought hopelessly.

There was to be a one-hour rest period before the personality tests. When Linda returned to the trailers she found Dona and Bronco there with Bob, Kathy, and Larry. "You rode like a real champ," said Bob. "And now tell us what happened. Why did you leave here?"

Briefly Linda explained, while her brother took care of Chica d'Oro. Everyone was speechless with fury and disgust at Shirley's trickery.

173

"She should be disqualified!" declared Bronco angrily.

Kathy, Bob, and Larry clamored to report the girl's actions to the judges. But Linda held them back.

"Please don't say anything to anybody," she begged. "The only way I want to get square with Shirley Blaine is by a fair riding contest."

Dona smiled at her granddaughter lovingly and said, "I'm proud that we have true nobility in our girl."

Linda kissed her, then said, "I'd better get into my outfit or I'll be going through the personality test still in jeans!"

"Top luck!" Bronco wished her.

Dona added, "We'll all go back to the grandstand now. I know you will perform well, my dear."

"Of course you will." Bronco gave Linda a reassuring pat.

As soon as the Mallorys had left, Kathy exclaimed, "Linda, you really must eat to put some pep into you. How do you expect to win a single point against well-fed, smug Shirley in the personality test if you're hungry, sad-faced, and angry? No argument. I'm going to get you a sandwich!"

Linda looked at Kathy and laughed for the first time in hours. "I see your point," she admitted. "I'll take your advice."

Kathy dashed to the caterers' trucks. Meanwhile Linda dressed in her sparkling green outfit and white accessories. By the time she was ready, Kathy had returned with a chicken sandwich and a glass of milk.

After she had eaten Linda stood up and stretched. The natural sparkle had returned to her eyes and the glow to her cheeks.

"I feel like a million!" she exclaimed, looking with deep fondness at Bob and her two friends, and added huskily, "You're all so wonderful to stand by me. You know, I feel as if I just might win that personality test. At least, I'm going to try mighty hard!"

The others smiled, thinking there was a positive aura of radiance about her now.

"You can't miss, Linda," declared Larry admiringly. "You look terrific."

The call came over the loud-speaker: "Queen contestants enter!"

Linda walked with Larry, Kathy, and Bob to the grandstand. Then, while the three went up to take seats, she joined the other girls in the boxes reserved for them.

Valerie Vance, owner of a modeling school, was to be the judge for the personality contest, and Mrs. Freeman, wife of one of the horse show judges, Hal Freeman, sat at a table to engage the girls in brief conversations.

Each girl was to walk for a certain distance in front of the grandstand, then turn and walk back. Next she would pose for a picture, and finally sit at the table for a few minutes talking with Mrs. Freeman.

"This is going to be lots harder than riding," murmured one of the contestants, and the others nodded in agreement.

During the test Linda held her white gloves casually in her left hand as she had once seen the wife of a commanding officer do at an important military function.

Shirley Blaine did not remove her gold lamé gloves and tightly clasped her hands together now and then. Otherwise she was well poised and outstanding with her beauty.

The applause from the grandstand was generous for even the most nervous girls. It was therefore impossible for Linda and her fellow contestants to guess how things were going.

That evening there was to be a queen's banquet for the girls and their families. At eight o'clock the announcement of the winner and her four princesses would be made, after the judges and committee had computed all of the points.

A large marquee had been erected for the banquet —featuring delicious roast squab. The girls were too excited to have much appetite, but a comedian and lively strolling musicians who had been engaged to relieve the tension largely succeeded in doing so.

At Linda's table, Kathy and the boys tried to divert their friend by nonsensical banter. Linda laughed gaily when Larry asked with a straight face, "Is this a coo-coo squab?" and Kathy retorted, "Anyway, it's not a cuckoo bird."

At a quarter to eight Mort Sullivan, president of the Trail Blazers organization, appeared and immediately conversation ceased. The air became electric with anticipation. Linda's pulse throbbed rapidly and a tingle went up her spine. The judges' decision was about to be announced!

Mort began, "There is a tie between two contestants. It has been decided by the committee to break it through a horsemanship contest between the two. Will Shirley Blaine and Linda Craig please ride into the arena at eight o'clock?"

There followed a burst of excited babbling, and Shirley's mother was heard to exclaim, "Not that ranch girl in jeans! Why, I never heard of such a thing!"

Linda was stunned speechless, but Kathy hugged her, crying joyously, "You'll win! I just know it!"

Linda smiled as the others showered her with congratulations and wishes for success. Her other winning points had made up for those lost on costume!

"Well, my dear," said Dona softly, "at least *you* will be riding with a clear conscience."

"I'll get Chica d'Oro ready," Bob offered, rising.

Linda dimpled. "Thank you, brother," she replied. "You are a first-class groom, and I appreciate it. But

I'd like to have a little visit with my golden girl before this particular contest."

"I understand."

Linda hurried off. The palomino welcomed her with a pleased whinny.

"Chica," said Linda earnestly, "you and I have a great challenge to meet. We'll do it, won't we, baby?"

Chica responded by whinnying again and nuzzling her mistress.

"I knew you'd agree!" Linda said and hugged the filly.

At eight o'clock the spectators were back in the grandstand. Linda and Shirley sat their horses side by side at the arena entrance, waiting for the command to come in. Shirley appeared furious and refused to look at Linda, who wore a continuous, pleasant smile.

When the two girls were called in, they were requested to repeat their performances of that afternoon. Linda and Chica were at the peak of perfection, and made a scintillatingly beautiful picture under the bright floodlights of the arena.

Linda observed that Shirley tightened up again in her truculence, and the Arabian acted confused and hesitant a couple of times in its response to her commands. Despite this they executed an exceptionally fine performance.

The two girls were called to the judges' box and instructed to dismount. Bob, who was standing by, took Chica, and Shirley's groom was handed the Arabian's reins. The girls remained where they were to hear the result.

Linda was outwardly calm and poised. In reality her knees felt shaky and every nerve was taut. Shirley held herself rigid, staring straight ahead.

Judge Freeman looked over his notations. Then he wrote a name on a small slip of paper and handed it to Mort Sullivan who stood at the mike. A dramatic silence had fallen over the crowded grandstand.

The Trail Blazers president smiled at the audience, then announced, "Well, here we have the news that you've all been waiting to hear. The name of the winning queen is—Linda Craig of Club 28."

The Club 28 membership went wild, and thunderous applause came from everyone else except those in the Malibu Club.

Shirley's face registered deep shock. She did not say a word to her victorious rival.

"And now the names of the princesses," Mort Sullivan continued. Shirley Blaine was named first, then three other girls.

Shirley's groom stepped over to her, and Linda heard him say in a British accent, "I did my best to help you win, Miss Shirley."

Linda studied the groom speculatively. He was tall and thin, and had a small black mustache.

Suddenly Shirley said brusquely to him, "I'm getting out of here!" She stepped into the saddle and rode quickly out of the arena.

"Miss Blaine, come back here or you will be disqualified!" called one of the committeemen. But the girl did not comply.

Mort Sullivan spoke quickly to the judge, who consulted his list, to select another princess in Shirley's place. The new name announced was that of Jill Raymond, the petite black-haired girl. She jumped up and down in excitement and burst into happy tears.

The magnificent queen's trophy was presented to Linda, and an enormous sheaf of red roses placed in her arms. The congratulations and praise of all the officials were lavish, and the applause of the crowd was genuine and loud.

Trophies were also awarded to the princesses. Flashbulbs popped continuously as pictures were taken of Linda and the runners-up. Families and club members clustered about the winners.

"It's all so wonderful!" exclaimed Linda. "Like a dream. But I never could have won without Chica d'Oro's help."

Finally Dona and Bronco left to return home. Linda, Bob, Larry, and Kathy returned to the trailers. Linda took a few seconds to show Chica the big trophy, hugged and praised her, and gave the filly a red rosebud to eat.

Suddenly the new queen turned to the others and said, "I believe I know who the mystery man is!"

"What?" Bob cried. "Sis, don't keep us in suspense!"

"Shirley Blaine's groom," was Linda's surprising answer. "He's tall, thin, has a black mustache, and I heard him tell Shirley he had done his best to help her win."

"But the English accent?" Bob protested.

"I believe he just uses that for effect," said Linda.

"We'd better hotfoot it over to the Sierra Stables before he disappears," Bob urged.

The four drove there and asked at the office for Miss Blaine's groom.

"That would be Ferd Fenwick," said the man in charge.

Linda, Kathy, and the boys quietly approached the building where the horses were kept. They slipped inside and spotted Ferd Fenwick. He was talking with several other grooms. Drawing closer, they heard him speaking.

"Just as I suspected!" Linda whispered. "Ferd Fenwick has no British accent. I'm convinced that he is the one who tried to drown me, loosened the trailer wheel, trapped us on the trail, and used the beard disguise to kidnap us at the fair!"

Without hesitation Bob called out, "Mr. Fenwick, we want to ask you some questions."

The tall man turned away from his companions and sauntered toward them. "Well, what is it?" he demanded impatiently.

181

Linda stepped forward and made her accusations. The groom's face contorted with rage and his lips drew back in a snarl. Suddenly he lunged at Linda as if to choke her.

XV

An Ancestor's Revelation

As Fenwick lunged at Linda, Bob and Larry leaped forward to block him. The groom fought the two boys with savage thrusts. Although he was thin, the man's muscles were like steel.

Bob's fist lashed out and caught Fenwick squarely on the jaw. He staggered backward and Larry hastily pinioned his arms. Quickly Bob whipped a leather strap from a hook on the wall and tied Fenwick's wrists together.

"Ready to talk?" Bob snapped.

By now the other grooms had run over and were staring in stupefaction. "What's going on?" one asked.

"This man is guilty of attempted murder and kidnaping," Larry replied hotly. "Will you please call the sheriff?"

The man stared, dumfounded. "Right away!" he gulped, and hastened to the office.

The other two grooms, evidently unnerved, and not wishing to become involved, quickly made their departure. Seeing that he was definitely trapped, Fenwick's belligerence ebbed away. He asked in a whining tone, "You going to file all those charges against me?"

"We have no choice," replied Bob sternly.

Linda faced the captive. "You may as well admit everything," she advised. "How did it happen that a fine groom like you, employed by prominent people, became associated with a man like Hank Trask?"

"Known him for years," replied Fenwick. "He used to work at the stables and wasn't particular what he did to make a fast buck. I've kept in touch. He knew tricks to knock out horses. Picked them up at race tracks where he hung out a lot. I paid him to have Rod Coleman thread your horse's legs."

"But Shirley Blaine is a first-class horsewoman, and has fine horses," said Linda. "Her chances to win were good."

Fenwick gave Linda a slanting glance. "You know better. I was afraid you'd be a threat to Miss Shirley's chances in the club's horse show if you made the Trail Blazers. So I figured out various ways to prevent your becoming a member."

Kathy looked aghast. "How awful!" she cried. "Winning a contest isn't worth doing all those dreadful things."

"For me it was," declared Fenwick. "Miss Shirley

has highfalutin contacts. If she'd won the competition today, she was in line to be asked to join the Olympic equestrian team. This would help *me* go on to bigger and better shows."

"In other words," Linda said in disgust, "your schemes to put me out of the running were for your own selfish ends."

Fenwick's eyes took on a maniacal glitter. "It would've been a swell deal," he said, "going along with Miss Shirley in the Santa Barbara Olympic workouts, Chicago's International show, the finals in Scarsdale, New York—and then on to the Olympic games." The groom gritted his teeth. "I would've hit the big time—if you pests hadn't wrecked everything."

The prisoner admitted that Shirley had feared Linda's competition, but had not been part of any of the attempts to harm Linda or Chica d'Oro. The Malibu girl had mainly wanted to prevent her rival from appearing in the queen's contest.

Fenwick further confessed to being guilty of all Linda's accusations, including the attempt to drown her. He had stalked the young trail blazers to the beach, carrying his skin-diving equipment. The groom had donned swim trunks, hidden behind a large rock a short distance away, and watched for his chance to harm Linda.

"Too bad you all didn't fall into that camouflaged pit I set up near the fallen tree," Fenwick added.

"I suppose you rigged up the desert detour too," Bob said coldly.

"That's right," the groom replied insolently.

Linda next quizzed him about his tie-in with the Coleman brothers. Fenwick snorted. "Hardly knew them—they're Hank's cronies. But the one called Rod came in handy at the fair. He wanted your old family jewels enough to help me get you away. I was going to keep you locked up some place until after the Cowboy Park show."

"You also had someone phone a fake message about closing time for the Trail Blazers entries," Linda charged.

This, however, Fenwick flatly denied. "You'll have to figure that one out," he said sullenly. Linda felt sure now that the mysterious female caller had been Shirley Blaine.

The next moment a police car roared up and several deputies jumped out. Fenwick was quickly handcuffed and, after the Craigs had made a brief statement to the lawmen, was driven off.

Linda turned to the others. "Everybody had enough excitement," she asked with dancing eyes, "or shall I dig up some more—like finding the Perez jewels?"

Larry grinned. "No thank you, Queen Linda! Although I'm sure you could!"

Early next morning the four new Club 28 members

set out for home. They were in a festive mood, still jubilant over Linda's triumph. Upon reaching del Sol, she was given an enthusiastic reception by everyone at the ranch.

"Yippee-ki-oo!" shouted Cactus Mac, throwing his ten-gallon hat into the air. "We're mighty proud o' our queen. And sure as shootin', you'll be winnin' another crown one o' these days on that thar purty little filly o' yours." Then he sobered. "I guess even better'n beatin' that uppity gal was catchin' those varmints."

"I'm glad," said Linda. "It worried me that I was the cause of so much trouble to all of you."

Cactus turned to Bob. "Got some good news. We just heard from the sheriff where the Colemans hid your coin collection. He's sending men to get it."

"Swell!"

Luncheon was an extra-special affair, for Luisa had prepared some fine dishes for the celebration. Afterward Linda drew her grandmother aside in the hall.

"Dona," she said, "I'm still curious about the young woman who made that hoax phone call. Was there anything unusual in the way she spoke?"

Mrs. Mallory reflected for several moments. "I do recall," she replied, "the person had an odd way of pronouncing Rancho del Sol. I believe she said, 'de la Sol.'"

"I was right," Linda murmured. "Shirley Blaine

was the culprit. But," she went on, "I won't pursue the matter. Shirley's had her punishment, I guess."

Dona agreed. Then, smiling, she handed her granddaughter a large square envelope. "This came for you yesterday. I have a feeling it's an invitation."

Linda noted that it was postmarked Santa Barbara, where the most famous and colorful of all southern California fiestas is held. She observed with shining eyes the Old Spanish Days return address in the corner. Invitations, she knew, were sent only to well-screened and selected riders.

Excitedly she opened the envelope, and took out two pieces. One was a beautiful formal parchment invitation to ride in El Desfile Historico, the Old Spanish Days historical parade. There would be La Cabalgata, an equestrian promenade to socialize on horseback as in the old days, and a California Royal Rancho pageant to be presented in the Santa Barbara bowl.

The other paper was a personal letter to Linda from Anthony Trent, the parade chairman, inviting her, as a notable descendant of one of California's first Spanish families, to act as the bride in the wedding party, a most important feature of the parade.

"How thrilling!" Linda murmured, awestruck by the honor. "How wonderfully thrilling!" Then she puckered her forehead and said, "But if I accept I would have to wear a beautiful wedding dress."

Linda turned her gaze toward the portrait of Rosalinda Perez and murmured softly, "I'll be riding with the descendants of many of the first grandee families whom you knew."

Then a striking thought came to her. Linda said slowly, "Dona, do you suppose—I might wear Rosalinda's wedding dress, if I took good care of it?"

Dona beamed lovingly upon the girl and replied, "I don't know of a more appropriate use for the dress, dear. Suppose you try it on."

"Oh, thank you!" cried Linda, and ran to the carved chest to take out the ancient gown.

She raised the heavy lid, and held up the exquisite white silk brocade and lace wedding dress with its long tight bodice and bouffant skirt with many yards of lace flouncing. Linda gathered it in her arms and hurried to her room. Soon she returned attired in the gown.

"How do I look, Dona?" she asked breathlessly, turning about slowly for her grandmother's appraisal.

Mrs. Mallory smiled warmly. "You make a lovely picture indeed. I see the bodice is somewhat long, however. It will have to be shortened."

"I'll alter it right now!" Linda ran to change and came back with her sewing basket. She sat down on the living room couch with the beautiful dress spread around her. Eagerly she ripped a well-bound seam at the waist.

189

Two ruby pendants and an emerald ring rolled out!

"Jewels!" Linda cried. "Rosalinda Perez's lost jewels!"

"How amazing!" exclaimed Dona.

Excitedly Linda ripped other seams. Each revealed jewels, until there was heaped before her a wealth of pearls, rubies, diamonds, and emeralds.

Linda, almost dazed by her discovery, said in awe, "To think that all this time they really *were* hidden in the chest!"

At that moment Bronco and Bob strode into the room and stared unbelievingly at the scene.

"Rosalinda Perez's jewels!" Linda told them and Dona explained the find.

All four were radiant with joy until suddenly Linda's face clouded. "That awful Hank Trask!" she exclaimed in dismay. "We will have to give him his share."

Bronco slapped his thigh. "I forgot to tell you!" he said. "I had a talk with the sheriff. It seems Trask broke down and confessed he'd faked the paper he left in Chica's stall. He had read the story of the missing jewels in the museum, saw the original letter there, and copied it. The Perez jewels belong to the Rosalinda namesakes of your great-great-grandmother."

Linda arose and went to gaze at the portrait. Smiling, she said, "How clever of you to hide the jewels in your wedding dress, Great-Great-Grandmother! Somehow you must have known we finally would discover the secret of Rancho del Sol!"

E20

Linda and Chica d'Oro